STARS & STEEL

NICOLE KNAPP

Edited by Kassie Metivier and Gretchen Davison

Cover Design by Shayne Leighton

Parliament House Press

www.parliamenthousepress.com

To the ones who left me in the darkness; this is what came out of it with me.
Thank you.

PROLOGUE

Elena was not the first student to disappear from the academy. There had been a few before her, mostly girls around Elena's age but the occasional boy as well. Elena was the first to return, though. The headmaster was not sure where the students were taken. The only thing that the disappearances seemed to have in common were the open windows left behind in their rooms.

When Henry accepted the position as headmaster at the academy, he had been warned that something sinister surrounded the school. Upon his arrival, Henry was instructed to make sure that all windows remained closed "for the protection of the students." That was the only information he ever received about the situation. Henry practically scoffed at the warnings. He did not believe them; he simply chalked it up to silly superstition. When the first girl under his watch disappeared, no one noticed for almost a week. Her name was Wendy.

As soon as it was brought to his attention, Henry had gotten the authorities involved of course. He was even considered a suspect for some time, but eventually was cleared. Days passed with no trace of Wendy, days then turned into weeks, then into months, but there was no sign of the girl. Guilt tore at the headmaster for years after her disappearance. When it happened again, Henry almost lost it completely. It was a boy that disappeared that time; he was only twelve years old. After the second occurrence, the headmaster became obsessed with preventing the disappearance of any more children from his school.

Henry's obsession got so bad that he let everything else go. It got to the point that the academy itself began to fall into disarray. The closed windows mixed with London's damp climate caused the entire building to develop a strange smell, and over the years all the building's repairs fell to the side as the headmaster's obsession grew. Henry could sense the scorn of the instructors; he saw the way they looked at him, with a mix of pity and disgust. He lost quite a few wonderful employees because of the state of the building and the missing students. But he could not stop. Henry was very thorough as he researched similar disappearances. A pattern emerged: every three years, a child would disappear from somewhere around the world. Most of the disappearances occurred throughout Europe and the United States, but there were some instances in Australia, New Zealand, China, and Japan. Henry also discovered another similarity: many of the missing children seemed to be orphans or had very few close living relatives. Of course, there was no way to know for sure if all of the disappearances were related, or what actually became of the children, but Henry certainly had his theories. And then his own niece was the one to go missing, right after her arrival in London. When he attempted to check in on her to see how she was adjusting, he had found only an empty room and an open window and knew immediately what had happened. The headmaster knew this was the year a child would go missing, but he had hoped that his school would be spared this time, though it made him feel awful to think such things.

The headmaster hesitated to get the authorities involved once more, afraid that he would once again be a suspect. He was so tired of answering the same questions and receiving the same scrutiny each time a student went missing. He told himself that no one would even know that she was gone, as he was the only family she had. He knew what a horrible person those thoughts and actions made him. But then Elena reappeared, and Henry was so relieved. She did not show up alone though. Elena brought with her a young man, rugged but still handsome, with a strange accent. The young man, Will, did not seem to fit in, and once again the headmaster had his theories.

Henry should have turned Will out. He should not have allowed him to reside in the school with his niece, but Elena seemed so enamored by Will that Henry could not bring himself to do so. He felt that after his inappropriate thoughts and actions, that he owed it to his niece to allow her young man to stay. He felt that he owed it to her to allow her to find happiness, and Will seemed to make her happy. So, the headmaster bit his tongue about the strange situation, vowing to himself that he would do whatever he could to ensure that Elena lived a happy and safe life.

Because Elena was the first to ever return, Henry suspected that she had escaped from wherever she had been. Henry did not trust that Will would be enough to keep Elena safe. He could not resist offering a cryptic warning upon her reappearance, in the hopes that she would keep her guard up. Because if she did escape, then whoever took her could come for her again. And deep down Henry knew that it was not over.

CHAPTER 1

The sheets are soaked with sweat when I jolt awake. It's happened every night since I returned from Neverland. The same thing, night after night, with no reprieve. Nightmares so realistic that I can smell the scorched wood of the burning Jolly Roger, hear the terrible sound of fairies being shredded apart by mermaids, feel the blood on my skin. My blood, Will's, Aiden's. So much blood, hot and sticky, gushing from around the hilt of a dagger and onto my hand.

He appears in my dreams most often. Aiden. I see his green eyes, strangely bright and hypnotic. They draw me in as he smiles at me. Then he tells me he is going to kill me. And that is usually when I wake, soaked in my own sweat, gasping for air. But he can't hurt me anymore; Aiden can't kill me, because he is already dead. I killed him. I shoved a dagger into his heart. I watched the light leave those strange eyes as his life slipped away.

Will says that he does not hold his brother's death against me. He says that it had to be done, that there was no other way, it was either Aiden or me. Will is so good to me, always comforting and reassuring me when I am falling apart, even though he is struggling too. But no matter how loved he makes me feel, I know that he loved his brother too.

What happened in Neverland will likely haunt the both of us forever. How could it not? The events that occurred over those weeks, both good and bad, will be ones we will never be able to forget. One thing I know for sure though: I will *never* go back there.

The boy paces the short length of his tree house. Outside, lightning cracks across the dark sky. It has not stopped storming since he returned to Neverland. *My own fault*, he muses. Since he failed to harvest the girl's youth, his magic has been greatly diminished and what remains is erratic and hard to control. The instability of his magic and emotions could be catastrophic for Neverland.

Thunder booms in the distance, so loud it reverberates in his bones. He must find a way to regain his power, to stabilize it, and he must do so quickly, before it destroys him entirely.

The pirate rolls over and breathes in the scent he has come to love. Lavender and something sweeter. Vanilla, maybe? He could breathe her in forever and never tire of that smell. Her auburn hair is splayed across the pillow, her breathing deep and even. He envies her ability to sleep, even if she does still have the dreadful night terrors that wake her so often.

Will has not slept for more than a few hours in the days since coming to this world. No matter how hard he tries, sleep eludes him. The images burned into his memory are too strong to allow him sleep. Ruby blood, pumping onto the sandy floor of a cave, the black tendrils of malice being cast into a fire, a burning ship in the dark, the woman he loves lying on a stone altar in that same cave. Those images will never stop haunting him.

Elena rolls toward him, her head coming to rest just over his heart. She sighs through her nose before her breathing evens out once more. The pirate wraps his arms around her and pulls her close. He closes his eyes and waits for the nightmares to come so he may chase them away for her.

I wake in the morning to the smell of salt and wind. Despite the nightmares last night, a small smile tugs at my lips. It seems impossible that Will could still smell like the sea. Maybe it is in his blood. I asked him, more than once, if he regrets his decision to leave Neverland. "I do miss the sea, my ship," he told me, "but I would have missed you more had I stayed."

The same response, every time. And every time it melts my heart. But I can see the strain on his handsome face, the dark smudges that seem to be permanent beneath his eyes. I know coming here has taken its toll on him. I know he is not sleeping, and yet night after night, he comforts me when the nightmares tear me from sleep. I wish there were something I could do to help him, but I do not know what.

Will barely leaves my room, well, our room I suppose. He is constantly preoccupied with thoughts of the future, with finding work and providing for himself, and me as well. All of that mixed with adjusting to this world, it has him in a downward spiral. As odd as it may sound considering what we went through in Neverland, things were easier there. We meshed so well together, we got along, we were happy being together. Here, it is all stress and bickering and nightmares.

It has crossed my mind that maybe we should have just stayed in Neverland. Thanks to the way time moved and the island's magic, we would have stayed young for a long time, and we would have no worries about the future or money or jobs or school. The island would have provided everything we needed. But then I picture the blood pulsing over my hand, I *feel* it, sticky and hot on my fingers, and those thoughts are chased away in an instant. Often I do wonder what happened to the Lost Children though. Are they alright? Are the fairies caring for them? Surely they are better off now that *he* is gone...

Will and I do not speak of him often, and when we do, we don't say his name. It has become a taboo in our relationship. I am not stupid though. I know that his brother haunts his thoughts.

"My uncle wants to have dinner with us tonight," I say, breaking the heavy silence in the room. Standing in the tiny bathroom, I can practically *feel* Will stiffen in the other room. Dragging a brush through my hair, I turn to lean against the door frame. "You have to get to know him eventually, Will." I know he is not looking forward to it, but my uncle is the only family I have.

"Aye," Will scrubs at his face with both hands. "Can you blame me for putting it off though?"

I cross my arms over my chest, but a smile tugs at my lips. "No, but let's just get it over with."

"As you wish, love," he sighs. His voice is resigned, a deflated version of the rough yet melodic voice I love so much. It is just another sign of his unhappiness. He tries to act and sound normal, like himself. But I know him far too well to fall for the act. He can't fool me.

To top everything off, my Uncle *knows*. I do not know how much he knows exactly, or how he could possibly know, but he *knows*. A couple of days after I got back, Uncle Henry called me into his office as I was walking past.

"Elena," he began. "Where were you really these past few days?"

I had protested, insisted I hadn't gone anywhere. He had given me a knowing look.

"I went into your room looking for you," he said. "The window was open."

I ducked my head to hide the blush burning in my cheeks.

"I warned you, Elena," he continued. "Nothing good comes from open windows. They only invite strange people in, and strange people can lead you to strange places."

I sucked in a breath, unable to conceal my shock.

Uncle Henry gave me that same knowing look then pushed his spectacles up his nose.

"Perhaps you learned your lesson," he said before turning his attention back to the stack of documents on his desk.

Swallowing against the lump in my throat, I nodded and practically ran out of his office.

How could it be possible for Uncle Henry to know about Aiden and Neverland? Was I not the first person to disappear from the school? Has Uncle Henry seen or met Aiden? The wheels in my head began to turn, connecting dots I had not even noticed until now. I had so many questions I wanted to ask, but at the time I could not find my voice, or maybe I was just too scared to hear the answers.

I have only seen my Uncle a handful of times since that encounter, but he has not mentioned my disappearance since, or hinted about any of it, so I acted like nothing happened as well, but the unanswered questions still burn in my mind. It never occurred to me that some of Aiden's other victims could have come from this school. I suppose I had assumed that Aiden just chose his victims at random. The more I thought about it though, it made sense for Aiden to target the same places. I mean, it's not like anyone could catch him in Neverland.

Will does not know about any of it; I never told him about the strange conversation with my uncle. I should tell him, but I feel like it would only make him feel more self-conscious around my Uncle and all I want is for the two of them to get along. I'll tell him, I will, when the time is right...

That evening, hand in hand, Will and I descend the staircase to meet my uncle. We both stop suddenly at the sight of a familiar head of honey colored hair at the bottom. Cash. Guilt tears at my insides and Will's hand tightens around mine. Cash is a large sore spot in our relationship. Understandable, considering that the night Will arrived in my world, I was out with Cash.

As if the tension between Will and I is not bad enough, things with Cash certainly are not wonderful. We have barely spoken two sentences to each other since Will arrived and I told Cash that I could not see him again. And now when we cross paths, he turns away without any acknowledgement of my existence.

The day after Will showed up in my room, a knock at the door woke me. When I opened the door to find Cash standing there with two cups of coffee in his hands and a smile on his face, it made me want to sink through the floor. It was even worse to watch Cash's smile fade when Will came up behind me, kissed my shoulder and asked, "Who is it, love?"

"Oh," Cash had said.

And then he turned and walked away, dropping both cups of coffee into a trashcan before turning the corner and disappearing from sight. The smug look on Will's face when I turned to him only spiked my temper.

"Stop smiling," I had snapped.

His face had fallen, but he recovered quickly, an angry look taking over his features instead.

"Why does it bother you? The boy clearly wants you; I was only showing him that his efforts are futile."

"It was unnecessary Will," I said, brushing past him and walking into the bedroom.

"Do you want him now? Is that it?" he demanded, following behind me.

"Don't be stupid, you know I only want you," I said. "But you didn't need to rub it in his face like that. I was going to tell him that we couldn't be together, I didn't need you to do it for me."

Will was quiet for a moment, his face unreadable. Turning away, I entered the bathroom and began brushing my teeth. When I finished and looked in the mirror, he was standing behind me.

Wrapping his arms around my waist, he met my gaze in the mirror. "I apologize love; I should not have interfered."

"No, you shouldn't have," I agreed, though my temper was already fading.

"It just bothered me to see him trying to take what is mine," he had said softly.

Turning in his arms, I wrapped my own around him. "But I am yours, that's not going to change," I said, pressing my lips to his.

That was the end of the fight, well, that particular one at least. The tension surrounding the three of us never seemed to fade though, and now, leading Will down the stairs, past Cash and towards my uncle's office, I can't stop the burning in my cheeks. I look down at my shoes to hide it from Will. I know he sees it though and it makes me feel even worse. I shouldn't care about Cash; I shouldn't worry about how he feels, but I do. My focus should be on Will, on making his adjustment to this world as easy as possible. I do care about all of that, of course, but for some reason I can't stop from caring about Cash.

When we round the corner, Uncle Henry is already waiting for us outside the door of his office. His hands are in his pockets, and while he wears his usual kind smile, behind the spectacles perched on his nose, there is wariness in his eyes.

"Uncle Henry," I greet him, trying to keep my voice cheerful as I lean up to kiss his cheek.

"Good evening, Elena, William."

The two men exchange a handshake, and with pleasantries aside, we head into the cold night. On our way out the door, I find myself glancing to where Cash was standing, but he is already gone. Something in my stomach tightens.

Will knows that Elena's uncle does not approve of him. He can see it in the man's eyes. But no matter how little the old man thinks of him, it cannot possibly be any worse than what Will thinks of himself. All he wants is to prove to Elena, Henry, and himself that he can be worthy of both respect, and Elena's love. He wants to prove that he is not just a pirate. He wants to prove that he is not uncivilized and plagued by darkness and the thirst for battle.

Then of course, there is the matter of the blond boy, the one Elena was with the night Will arrived in London.

He knows that nothing really happened between the two of them, but it does not mean that he and the boy will be friendly anytime in the foreseeable future. As the trio exits the school, Will notices Elena's head turn to where the boy had been standing. The boy is gone now, but as his hand tightens around Elena's, something heavy sinks in his stomach.

Dinner passed without any major issues. Will did wonderfully for someone who spent lifetimes living in Neverland and not in the modern world. Luckily for us, the conversation stayed light and Uncle Henry was great as well. He was polite, well mannered, gracious, and he did not so much as hint at his knowledge of the events surrounding my disappearance, or where Will was really from. Sitting at that table, I realized that Will is not the only one who does not know my uncle very well. As he spoke, telling little stories here and there, it dawned on me that Uncle Henry may be trying to get to know me as much as he is Will.

Back in our room, lying in bed with Will, I can't stop thinking about just how lucky I am to have him, to have someone to love like this. Will feels like home. When I am with him, it feels as though I could be anywhere, in any situation, and still be alright, as long as I am with him.

Rolling to my side, I lay my head on Will's chest. His familiar, strong heartbeat pounds against my cheek. His skin is warm and still somehow smells like the sea. He always smells of salt and wind and smoke, even after he has showered. I soak it all in, the smell, the rhythm of his heart. As my body begins to relax and sleep finally takes me over, it feels as though everything will be ok.

Far away, on an island in the middle of a vast blue sea, a boy with strange green eyes paces. The boy has laid his traps, he has placed his pawns, and he has chosen his players. A wicked, devilish grin spreads across his face. It is time.

At the edge of the room, the fairy hovers in midair, watching the boy pace about, her wings beating lightly behind her. The fairy thinks that even with such a menacing look on his face, the boy is still beautiful.

With his magic fading, the fairy has stepped up and done her part to help Aiden set his trap for the girl and his brother. She has spent each night outside the girl's window filling her and the pirate's heads with countless night-mares and images. Aiden's plan is clever, brilliant even. The fairy is proud to stand by his side.

CHAPTER 2

Something is not right.* It is the first thought to pop into my head when my eyes open. Sitting straight up, I quickly scan the room. One hand flies across the bed to rest on Will's chest. He wakes with a start, eyes wide and fearful. My other hand roams over my legs, arms, chest, neck.

"It was just a dream," I whisper into the darkness. More of a nightmare, but not real. It can't be real. There is no way that a certain green-eyed boy could be here. I know this because I killed him. Beside me, Will's breathing is heavy.

"What's wrong, what happened?"

"It was just a dream," I tell him, reassuring myself in the process.

Will sighs before lying back. After a few minutes his breathing evens out once more, sleep gripping him once again. I curl to my side and wiggle closer to his warmth, trying to shake the feeling of wrongness that refuses to leave me. For the rest of the night I do not sleep at all.

C lasses the next day are hell. I am so exhausted and plagued by the feeling of *wrong* that just staying awake is a struggle, much less concentrating on what my teachers are saying. All I can focus on is making it through my last class and having a long nap.

The room is empty and silent when I arrive back. No Will. My anxiety spikes until I notice the note on the bed. Only four words are written on the paper in his elegant, sprawling script. *Gone out, return soon.* My hands are shaking slightly, but he is safe. I am certainly not sleepy anymore though. Instead of the nap I was so looking forward to, I go out in search of a caffeine fix.

The café down the road makes the best lattes, which is probably why I go there almost every day, but their food is not bad either. Walking down the hallway, phone in hand and only half paying attention, I manage to dodge most of the students and faculty milling about. Just my luck though, at the top of the stairs I trip over my own feet and slam hard into someone. Even more my luck, that someone happens to be Cash.

"Crap, I'm sorry," I exclaim, righting myself.

"Maybe you should watch where you're going," Cash snaps before turning away to catch up with his friends.

"Cash, wait! I'm sorry, about everything." I hate the pain and neediness that comes through in my voice.

"It's cool, Elena. Just forget about it," he says dismissively.

"No, it is not cool!" I should really learn to quit while I

am somewhat ahead. I cannot stand the awkwardness any longer though. It is killing me.

"When I went out with you, I thought I was never going to see Will again. And then he showed up and...and I wasn't trying to lead you on or hurt your feelings," I say to his back. "Can we please just put it behind us and be friends?"

Cash doesn't even glance back at me. He stares straight ahead and says, "Really Elena, I don't care."

And then he is bounding down the stairs to his waiting friends. I know he was trying to hurt me. It worked. I deserve it, I really do. Still hurts though. But there is nothing more I can do about it. I tried. I put in the effort to make things better. That is all I can do. He will either come around, or he won't. I hope that he does.

The latte I down on the way back to school doesn't do much to combat my exhaustion. I am so tired by the time I reach my room that as soon as I sit down and find a comfortable position, I pass right out. My dreams are full of stars, the sea, darkness. Not exactly nightmares, but not entirely pleasant either. At some point Will returns home and lies down beside me, his arms snaking around me and pulling me close. I only stir slightly. Tonight, I do not dream of Aiden, and for that I am grateful.

The dinner with Elena's uncle had been eye opening for Will. He saw the fondness in Henry's eyes for her, though there was something else there too. Guilt maybe? But what would the man have to feel guilty for? Perhaps it was pity instead; he could just pity her situation. More than likely though, the man was only trying to hide his distaste for Will. He knows that Henry does not approve of him or their relationship, and why would he? Will has nothing to offer.

While Elena is in classes the following day Will sets out into the city. It is past time for him to learn his surroundings, and to learn the way this world works. He does not want to be a student at the school, but he does want to show that he is worthy of Elena. Will must find a way to provide for her in this world.

He finds himself at the Thames admiring the boats coming and going from the city and the sea. An idea forms in his mind. If Will can secure work aboard a fishing boat or something similar, he could provide a life for Elena *and* be close to the sea again. A smile forms on his face.

Despite the night's rest, the feeling of wrongness is still with me in the morning. Nothing seems amiss or out of place, but in my very bones I can feel that things are not as they should be. Will is still asleep when I leave for classes. I am glad that he is finally sleeping.

When I get back that afternoon though, he is gone again. It is somewhat frustrating, but I know he needs time and space to adjust and sort out everything in his head and in his heart. His whole life has changed because of me. Any normal person would need time to work through things. So, I keep myself occupied to distract from obsessing over what he is doing. It's Saturday, so I read and finish my homework. Then I clean the room and take a shower, but he still has not returned by the time I am done.

It is getting close to dinner time and my stomach is growling but I want to wait for Will. Settling in to study a bit for an exam I have coming up, I prop my feet up on the bed. The test is for biology, so the notes aren't exactly entertaining, but I immerse myself in them nonetheless. A sudden noise jolts me out of my concentration.

"Will," I call.

The late evening shadows are stretched eerily across the walls. There is no answer. An odd sense of déjà vu hits me. Strange noises, the feeling of something being off. No...

"Hello Elena."

The voice comes from the darkest corner of the bedroom. A voice like a silver bell. Tatiana. I am dreaming, I have to be. It is just another nightmare. Please let it be a nightmare...

"Bet you thought you would never see me again," the fairy giggles.

"I certainly hoped that I wouldn't," I reply as she steps out of the shadows.

A smirk appears on her face. "The feeling was mutual."

Her green eyes take me in. Bright, but not nearly as bright as Aiden's.I try to shake the thoughts of him from my mind. My breath catches in my chest as I picture his eyes going dim as he bleeds out on the sand.

"What do you want, Tatiana?" I manage to ask.

"It is not about what I want, for I do not want to be here," the fairy clicks her tongue. "It is about what has happened."

My heart jumps into my throat at her words. "Will?" I gasp.

"No, stupid girl," the fairy snaps. "Your pirate is safe, for now."

For now. Did she really just say *for now*? What the hell is that supposed to mean?

"What the hell is going on Tatiana?" My palms have gone sweaty; my heart is racing.

"I'm afraid I come bearing bad news," she says, examining her nails.

"Spit. It. Out," I hiss through clenched teeth.

The fairy shifts on her feet, her face gone suddenly serious. "Aiden is alive, Elena."

Time stops. My heart stops. The Earth stops rotating on its axis. No air is getting to my lungs.

"It seems as though he was more powerful than any of us knew," Tatiana continues.

"No. No, I-I killed him. I-"

"I'm afraid you did not. Aiden is very much alive, though he is quite weak," the fairy shrugs, as if she hasn't just cracked my world in half.

I am still struggling to get air to my lungs; they are on fire. Am I going to faint? The door bangs open, heavy footsteps echo through the other room. They stop at the bedroom door.

"What the *bloody hell* are you doing here, fairy?"

My body reacts at the sound of Will's voice. Air floods into my organs, my heart resumes beating. But with that reaction comes others. My hands begin to shake, sweat beads on my forehead.

"I see that my news has shaken you," Tatiana says, and it looks like she is suppressing a smile. "Unfortunately for you, there is more. He has taken a hostage with him to Neverland. A hostage I think you will want to retrieve." She actually winks at me as she says the last part. Now I am seeing red.

"What the hell is going on?" Will raises his voice.

"Will," I say quietly, calmly. "Aiden is alive."

CHAPTER 3

"No," Will mutters. "No!" His voice grows louder as he fully absorbs the news. "I watched him die. I watched him bleed out on the sand!" His shouts fill the room; I wouldn't be surprised if my neighbors heard him.

Flinching at his outburst, I turn to look at him. Those beautiful blue eyes are filled with...fear? Shock? The dark circles beneath them are more prominent than yesterday.

"It is true. He is very much alive," Tatiana shrugs.

Glancing from Will's face to the fairy's, I take a hesitant step in Will's direction. He tenses and I halt. Will blinks once, twice, then reaches out a hand toward me. Practically sagging with relief, I let him pull me into his embrace. His arms tighten around me and my trembling ceases. His warmth seeping into my bones calms my mind and my heart. That is, until I remember Tatiana's second bit of information.

"Who did Aiden take hostage?"

"Hmm?" she acts as though she did not hear me. She

floats in the air, hands rearranging her messy hair. Her coyness is enough to make me positively murderous.

"Don't be cute," I snap. "Who did Aiden take to Neverland as his hostage?" Will tightens his arm around me.

"Oh, that," she muses, crossing her arms over her chest. "A boy, he took a boy with him, though I do not recall his name. He was a handsome one though! Hair the color of honey."

My world stops all over again.

"Cash," I breathe.

"Oh, yes! That's it!" Tatiana claps with glee.

Will stiffens beside me. I can feel the tension radiating from his body. Cash may be a sore subject between us, but surely he can't fault me for being concerned. There is no telling what Aiden will do to Cash, or what he has already done.

"Is Cash still alive?" I don't know if I really want to hear the answer, but I have to know.

"He is," the fairy replies flippantly. "For now."

My eyes widen, my head snaps around. "We have to save him, Will."

Those blue eyes are shooting daggers at the fairy across the room, who is now twirling in circles as if she did not just threaten an innocent boy.

"Will?" I keep my voice low.

Cash has been taken to Neverland. He is trapped there with that psychotic, sadistic monster Aiden. Aiden could be torturing Cash as we speak. He could be attempting to sacrifice him like he did with me. As we stand here talking, Cash could be taking his last breath. Will still has not responded, his eyes are still on the fairy, unblinking and intense.

"Why?" I demand. "Why take Cash? What does Aiden want?" My voice is much louder than I intended it to be.

Tatiana sneers. "You already know the answer to each of those questions, Elena."

She is right, I do know the answers. I do not want to admit it, not to myself, not to anyone, but I know what Aiden wants. He wants me. Aiden is using Cash to lure me back to that hellhole of an island. The demon that I once referred to as an angel is playing with my emotions to lure me back...and it is working.

"If I return to Neverland, Aiden will let Cash go?" I ask Tatiana. It's pathetic, the way my voice trembles when I say it.

A malicious grin spreads across the fairy's face.

"Elena, don't you *dare* even begin to think about-" Will starts to interject, finally breaking his silence, but Tatiana cuts him off.

"If you return to Neverland, the *both of you*," the fairy's green eyes flick between Will and me. "Then Aiden will let the boy go. You have my word."

"You cannot trust her!" Will hisses through clenched teeth. "She has obviously been working with him the entire time!"

I drag my fingers through my hair. A headache has started to form right behind my eyes.

"Your word means nothing," I direct at the fairy. Then to Will, "I know I can't trust her, I'm not stupid. But what choice do I have?"

I take in his handsome face, the angles of his cheekbones, the bright eyes, and the dark circles that are seemingly permanent beneath them. His jaw is clenched; I can see the muscle twitching beneath a few days' worth of dark stubble. He may be struggling, disheveled, angry, but he is still the most beautiful man I have ever seen.

"You don't have to come with me, Will," I assure him. I don't want to do this alone. But I will if it will save the lives of two people. Those ocean eyes ignite like blue fire.

"Over my dead body will I let you go alone," he growls.

I open my mouth to speak, but Tatiana cuts me off. "It's settled then!" she claps.

Her voice sounds like a silver bell and I hate her. God, I hate her.

"It is far from settled, fairy!" Will shouts.

Placing a hand on his arm, I attempt to steady him, to calm him. "I have to go, Will. I cannot let Cash die because of me. Whether you stay or go is entirely up to you."

Will rips his arm away from me, taking two steps back. "Damn it all to hell, Elena!" He presses his palms into his eyes. "Why are you always so bloody set on getting yourself killed?"

He is scared for me. I can see it in his eyes and I can hear it in his voice, though he is trying to keep it hidden. Turning to face him fully, I soften my voice.

"Will," I take his hands in mine, "I have to go. I survived Neverland before. I can survive it again." His eyes soften only a fraction as he lifts my hands to his lips, brushing them lightly across my fingers.

"Barely, love," he whispers. "You barely survived." The way he is looking at me breaks my heart.

"I have to go, Will," I whisper back.

Will takes my hand in his. "When I got home, I was going to tell you that I had found work. Stupid of me to believe that things were looking up."

My heart aches. That's where he was all day then, looking for a job. "Will, I am so proud of you." He tries to brush me off but I place my hand on his cheek. "When we get back we can start our lives together, really move forward."

"*If* we make it back," he says with a sad smile. Before I can respond he pulls me to his side to face Tatiana.

"Get on with it then, fairy."

Her face is practically glowing with excitement. Oh, I *hate* her. She steps closer to us, palm full of the glowing green dust that will fly us to Neverland.

"But first," Will says, stopping her in her tracks.

Her face is frozen with puckered lips and she looks so ridiculous that a laugh threatens to bubble around my lips despite the situation we are in. Will holds up his hand, the hand that is really only a glove. A sly smile creeps across his face.

"Before you drag us back to hell, you are going to give me my hook back," he pauses to wink at me. "I cannot be without one of my best weapons."

All signs of happiness vanish from the fairy's sharp little features. She must have known he would request that, but from the look on her face, she was hoping it would slip his mind. Tatiana rolls her eyes dramatically. "If you insist, pirate." The fairy snaps her fingers and the glove is gone, a shiny silver hook now in its place.

Will admires his hook for a moment, polishes it on his shirt, turns his arm this way and that.

"Are you not satisfied, Captain?" Tatiana snaps, her patience clearly at its breaking point.

Will looks once more at the hook, both his favorite weapon and one of his greatest weaknesses.

"Alright then, on with it," he shoots her a lazy grin. It's all a show, nothing more than an act. It must be. Will knows that the fairy will report everything back to Aiden. Our every word, every expression and movement will all be analyzed. It must be a front so Tatiana will have nothing useful to tell Aiden. I saw the look in his eyes before: the panic, the rage, the fear. Even if this trip to Neverland does not kill us, it might still break us.

Tatiana wastes no more time. She showers us in the glowing fairy dust. It is not nearly as pleasant and dreamy as I remember it being the first time around. Or maybe Tatiana just doesn't care about her presentation like Aiden had when he lured me to Neverland. My feet lift from the floor, Will's hand tightens around mine as we rise together.

Tatiana snaps her fingers, shifts into her tiny fairy form and darts out the window. "On with it then!" she calls in a mocking tone.

I begin to drift toward the open window, but Will pulls me back, circling his arms around me. I suppress a shudder. Something about being held like this, floating in the air, it reminds me of the night at the fairy tree with Aiden. The look in Will's eyes, the urgency in his voice, snap me back to reality quickly though.

"I will not let anything happen to you, Elena," he says quickly. "I will make sure that you get off that island alive, even if it means I do not." He kisses me then, deep and slow and with so much feeling that tears sting my eyes and cause my throat to tighten.

"Together," I murmur onto his lips. "We leave Neverland together this time."

Will says nothing. He simply kisses me once more, just a quick brush of lips on mine this time, and I get the sense that he does not intend to make it off the island at all.

The night air is frigid. Goosebumps erupt across my flesh the second we are out the window. The feeling of déjà vu is overwhelming. Panic begins to rise in my chest. I do *not* want to go back to Neverland. My breathing turns shallow. I do not want to see Aiden again. I'm terrified to face him. I try to focus on Will's hand, warm and rough in mine. He is the only thing that will keep me grounded.

Speaking of the ground, it is very far away now. The city of London stretches beneath us for miles, nothing but a sea of flickering lights as we sail through the sky. How did I not notice how far we have flown already? The stars are growing much closer; I can feel the heat from them now. We are flying faster, headed straight for the second star to the right. I really don't want to do this.

The pirate hates flying. He does not enjoy the height, or the feeling of being out of control. He much prefers to keep his boots firmly on the ground, or even better, on the deck of his ship. The pirate squeezes the girl's hand, so small and cold in his. Part of him is frightened of going back to Neverland. The other part is thrilled. More than ready to see the sea, to be on the Jolly Roger. Oh, how he wants to be sailing the sea that he named himself king of. But he does not want to see his brother.

Someone is going to die in Neverland. That is certain. But he will be damned if it is the woman he loves.

The boy is practically bursting with joy. His plan worked so perfectly. He has the ideal bait, bait that he knew Elena's soft heart would not be able to resist. It was all so perfect. His favorite fairy went to fetch the girl and his bastard of a brother. They should be arriving anytime now, and the boy is terribly excited to play again.

CHAPTER 4

We are racing through the sky, so close now to our star that I feel as though I may burst into flame. Sweat is soaking the back of my shirt, beading on my forehead. I have done this twice before, but it still takes me by surprise. There is a flash of blinding light and we emerge into...not sunlight like my first trip, but a dark sky.

Rain slaps me in the face, lightning cracking dangerously close to our little group. The electricity in the air is palpable. The next strike is even closer and I scream. The smell of ozone burns my nose and goosebumps erupt over my whole body.

Tatiana drops suddenly, forcing us to follow. Thunder booms, shaking me to my bones. Even my teeth clack together. We are low enough to reach out and touch the sea, but the idea of doing so is not nearly as romantic as my first encounter. The Never Sea is black; churning white capped waves soak me as we fly through the darkness.

"We are not far," Tatiana shouts over her shoulder.

How does she know? I can't see anything through the

storm. Will squeezes my hand, so hard that I realize it's to get my attention. When I turn my head to look at him, his eyes are on my face and I immediately know that we are not going to follow Tatiana to the island. Will tugs at my hand, a signal. We begin to veer slightly off the course Tatiana is flying. We do so slowly, trying to ensure that she does not notice our deviation too soon. If she catches us trying to escape, there is no telling what she might do. I don't know how she knows where the island is, or how Will knows where the ship is, but we are heading for the Jolly Roger. I'm sure of it.

Tatiana is almost out of sight, her messy blonde hair barely visible through the darkness and the rain. We make a break for it, and in the distance, a tiny flicker of light appears in the blackness. Will grips my hand tighter and we rocket toward the light, toward the only safe place for us in Neverland.

Lightning strikes directly in front of us, so close that I can feel its heat. I scream and my hand slips from Will's. It's as if Aiden knows exactly where we are, like he's aiming his storm and his magic at us. Hell, he probably is doing exactly that. We are just pawns in his game and all of Neverland is the board on which we play. I can hardly make out Will's form through the black and the pelting rain. Without his hand in mine I feel very alone, and not at all sure where I am going. But there, up ahead, the light is growing nearer. Almost there, I'm almost there.

"Elena!" I hear Will's voice over the raging of the sea and the howling wind. "Keep going, we are close!" he reassures me.

A mass begins to take shape ahead of us, the outline of

the Jolly Roger becoming clearer. We are too low though, if we don't get higher, and fast, we are going to crash into the hull of the ship.

"Will! Pull up!" I scream over the crack of the lightning and the booming of the thunder. "We're too low, pull up!"

My throat strains against my cries. Will does not respond, I do not even know if he heard me. Praying to every deity I've ever heard of, I begin to rise into the sky and hope that I make it over the railing in time.

The deck of the ship is in sight now, but there is not a soul on it. I am dangerously close to not making it. At the last second, my shoe catches on the railing, sending me crashing head over heels onto the wooden deck. My knees bang against the dark, wet wood, followed by my head. Pain shoots through my body, flickers at the edges of my vision.

Then Will is there, his hands roaming over my legs, my arms, assessing the damage. He takes my face in his hands and kisses me there on the deck, the storm raging around us. Now my head is spinning for an entirely different reason. I'm breathless when he pulls away. Rain runs down my face, in rivulets off my lips. Those blue eyes are all I can see. Depthless and captivating and staring back into mine like I am the only thing that matters in the world. God, I love him.

"Captain!" a booming voice calls out from the quarters near the back of the ship.

I blink my eyes a few times, rain dripping from my lashes. The pain in my knees and my head come racing back as quickly as they vanished. Mr. Miles, the former first mate and current captain of the Jolly Roger, is standing in the doorway, his massive outline illuminated from behind. Will stands, pulls me to my feet and all but drags me into the dim interior of the captain's quarters. The men clasp each other's forearms, pulling each other into a friendly embrace. Despite the stuffy warmth of the room, I can't stop trembling.

"You have returned, Captain!" Miles smiles. Then a puzzled look crosses his features. "But why are you back?"

Will does not respond. He snaps instantly into captain mode and begins to give orders. "Mr. Miles, gather the crew, ready our weapons. Prepare for an attack."

To Miles's credit, he does not question Will's orders. He only says, "Aye Captain," and rushes out the door leaving us alone in the dimly lit room. Will turns to me, face set with determination. "Let's get you into some dry clothes, love. I fear we may have a long night ahead of us."

I am still trembling slightly, but I let Will help me out of my soaked clothes and into a dry shirt and pants just like what I wore aboard the ship my first time in Neverland. The white shirt is far too big so I tuck it into the brown pants, which are also a bit big, but it will do. At least I'll be able to move freely, to fight when I need to. Because there is no doubt that there will be a fight.

Taking a seat on the edge of the bed, I wait while Will strips off his own wet clothes. Closing my eyes, I roll my head from side to side in an attempt to relieve some of the tension in my neck. The headache forming behind my eyes doesn't help matters either. I want so badly to lay down and just sleep, but sleep is not an option at the moment. There is so much that needs to be done, top priority being figuring out how to rescue Cash from Aiden. It will be a miracle if we can pull it off.

"Y ou lost them?" the boy asks the fairy.

She does not respond, cannot even meet his eyes.

"You lost them!" he roars this time, so loud that birds take flight from all of the trees around them.

Every lost child in the clearing falls silent. The fairy only cowers against the wall of the treehouse, shaking with shame and fear.

"The storm-" she tries to say.

"Do not blame your incompetence on me, fairy!" the boy shouts.

The fairy's face flames at the impact of his words. She never wished to disappoint him. She must do better.

T he boy is full of so much rage that he feels as though he may burst. His little remaining magic churns like the sea in the distance, wild, untamed. It is just like the pair of them to cause problems, to make him react in such a manner that none of his companions will so much as look at him. The boy knows that his brother and those bloody pirates will be expecting him. The assault on the Jolly Roger will take some planning and the delay will cost him precious magic but rushing into it would be foolish.

He must think of a new plan. It must be just right, the perfect mix of clever and evil. *In the meantime, though, the boy thinks, maybe a trip to Skull Rock to play with my new toy will provide inspiration.*

~

Cash's mouth is as dry as the sand that fills his vision. He can't be positive, but from the number of sunrises and sunsets he has seen through the two large holes in the cave wall, he believes he has been here for about a week. All Cash knows for sure, however, is that hanging for so long by his wrists has caused his arms to go numb. There is so much pain in his body that he isn't even sure which of his wounds are the worst. Every one of his joints aches and every single inch of his bruised and battered body hurts.

A pair of bare, dirty feet appears in the sand. *He's back,* Cash muses silently. He does not need to see the boy's face to know it's him. The boy grabs a handful of Cash's hair and uses it to yank his head up painfully. Bright green eyes regard him casually as the boy tilts Cash's head from side to side. The all too familiar sting of a blade dragging across his skin causes Cash to suck in a breath through his teeth.

"Still alive I see," the boy chuckles.

If Cash had the energy left to care, the hint of amusement in the boy's voice would bother him, but in his current state, Cash mostly hopes that his captor will finally kill him this time. As the assault on his body continues, Cash closes his eyes. The pain brings back the memory of how he came to be in this place.

After his encounter with Elena, Cash was looking forward to a night of blowing off steam with his friends. He was in such a hurry to catch up with them; that maybe that's why he didn't see the attack coming. He was hit in the head from behind, then everything went black. When he came to, he was slung over someone's shoulder flying above the ocean. Cash was sure he had lost it, or that he had been drugged; he wasn't sure which scenario would be worse. And when his assailant descended upon a small island and chained Cash to a wall, he decided that he didn't really care how he came to be here, only how he would escape.

At first, Cash tried to ask questions. "Who are you? Why are you doing this?"

He must have repeated them a hundred times. The only response he ever received was laughter and mocking. His captor couldn't be much older than him, but the boy clearly had plenty of experience in the art of torture. When the boy left him, Cash screamed for help until his vocal cords failed him. He fought against his restraints until his wrists bled. No matter how hard he tried he couldn't get free, and help never came, only the boy. The boy came back again and again, and as the torture and mutilation of his body continued, Cash stopped caring about his questions, stopped caring about escape as well. Mostly, he just wished that it would end.

Brought back to the present by a particularly deep, painful slice down his side, Cash looks into the eyes of his captor. The sensation of his skin splitting beneath a blade elicits a hiss, but as much as he wishes he could fight back, he has neither the energy nor the will.

CHAPTER 5

As fingers brush my cheek, my eyes open to reveal Will hovering above me. I'm flat on my back on the bed, as if I simply blinked and fell asleep. That may actually have been what happened.

"How long was I out?" I ask Will, propping myself up on my elbows.

"Not long," he shrugs. "I didn't want to wake you, but we have matters to attend to."

I can't believe that I fell asleep. Stupid. I'm still exhausted, but retrieving Cash is more important than my needs. Outside, the storm is still raging. I can hear the thunder, the waves crashing against the hull of the ship. Offering me his hand, Will pulls me to my feet. Despite our current situation, when Will grins down at me, my insides melt. My cheeks warm and I look away. He drops my hand, turns and crosses the room. Sinking down into the chair behind his desk, he pulls on his boots and laces them up. Just in time too. Outside the cabin, a commotion has arisen. I scramble around the cabin looking for my own pair of shoes, all the while the commotion outside is growing steadily louder. Will throws open the door. All of the candles gutter at the sudden rush of wind tearing through the room. I can hear the crew shouting, clambering about the ship.

"Will, what's happening?"

He looks back at me, I can see the fear beneath his swagger, beneath the mask he puts on for his crew and his enemies. Ice forms in the pit of my stomach.

"My sword, Elena," his voice is more calm than I expected. "Quickly, it should still be in the chest by the bed. Arm yourself as well. Sword, daggers, whichever you prefer," he instructs.

I do as he says. Something bad is going to happen; I can feel it. Will flicks his fingers in my direction. I toss the heavy sword to him, his good hand snatching it out of the air with practiced precision. Quickly rifling through the chest, I arm myself with a dagger and a smaller, shorter sword which I slip through the loop on my pants. Rising, I grab a dagger for Will as well and hurry to his side. Together we step out into the storm. The shouting has quieted some and the whole crew seems to be gathered around something.

"Move aside men!" Will bellows, taking my hand and pressing through the men until we get to the center.

There, surrounded by the entire crew, is Aiden. He is standing casually on the deck of the Jolly Roger, a wicked smile on his face and that same rudimentary crown atop his head. His eyes find mine instantly. The impact of seeing him again is...it's too much. As soon as his green eyes lock onto mine I stop breathing. It takes me a minute to realize that Aiden is not alone.

Cash is on his knees, back towards Aiden, who has Cash's golden hair gripped in one fist. Cash's face is bruised, bloody, streaked with dirt and tears. Various gashes and slices crisscross his bare torso; blood is slowly leaking down his chest. To top it all off, Aiden has that beautiful jeweled dagger held at Cash's throat. I take a step forward, then another. Will grabs me by the arm, preventing me from going any further. Cash's attention is on me, his eyes so full of hatred that my heart shatters like glass inside my chest. A strangled gasp escapes me as I stumble back into Will's chest. He grips my arm even harder.

"Lovely to see you, Elena," Aiden croons, that poisonous smile gleaming even in the darkness of the storm. Aiden's hair is soaked, hanging in little curls over his face. He looks wild, crazed.

"Aiden," I say, my voice little more than a whisper. "Let him go."

Those green eyes and the matching stones in his crown flash at the same time and lightning strikes the waves mere feet from the Jolly Roger. "No," Aiden smiles, "I don't think I will. You see, I am quite enjoying my new plaything."

Cash shudders. My eyes snap to him instantly and I have to resist the urge to rush to him. His eyes are closed now; his hair looks darker in the rain and is plastered to his skull. I can see him shaking, his skin slightly blue from the cold.

"Why are you doing this?" I ask.

Resentment and hate fill those strange green eyes.

"I am doing this," Aiden sneers. "Because you refused to be my queen, Elena. Because instead of staying with me like a good girl, you ran away."

He is lying. He could easily find some other unlucky girl to sacrifice and restore his magic. This is entirely personal now, a vendetta against me. That thought sends my heart stuttering. My mouth opens, closes, opens again. I imagine I look a little like a fish out of water. There are so many thoughts going through my head, but I can't seem to put together a sentence. Will speaks before I do.

"No, brother," he hisses. "You are doing this because Elena has deprived you of the magic you are so dependent on." He pauses, presses his lips to my hair. "That, and the small fact that she chose me over you."

Will is fronting again, but it has the effect he was going for. The look of pure rage on Aiden's features is priceless. I can feel the pirate swagger radiating from Will. He is such a good actor it's almost scary. I have never seen him look more like a pirate, except maybe the night we met.

Aiden's voice comes out as a hiss. "Is that right, *brother*?"

Will pulls me closer, his arm wrapping around my waist. "It does look that way, as I am the one at her side."

The whole scene has turned into once big pissing contest between the two brothers and my patience is beginning to wear thin. I am soaked to the bone and freezing which isn't helping matters at all. Cash is still staring intently at me; beneath the anger in his eyes there is also pain and fear. We need to get him away from Aiden *now*.

"Enough!" I shout. I did not mean to yell, to act like a

child. "Enough," I say again, my voice at a normal level this time. "Will, stop trying to piss off your brother," I order. "And Aiden, just tell us exactly what you want and quit playing games."

Both men look at me as though I have lost my mind, but I am done with the nonsense. I risk a glance at Cash. His skin is definitely going blue from the cold. There is a long pause, a moment where all I can hear is the snapping of the sails in the wind, the creaking of the ship as it rocks back and forth in the churning waves.

"As you wish, love," Will finally gives me a small nod. I nod back before turning to face Aiden and putting on my own front.

My arms are crossed over my chest, one hip popped out, eyebrows raised in question. Aiden lowers the dagger from Cash's throat.

"You are such a bore, the whole lot of you," he sighs dramatically. "But alright, have it your way."

Will and I say nothing, neither of us react. That is the best way to get to Aiden, I have learned.

He pauses again, but not for long.

"Give me my magic. I deserve it, I am owed it, it is mine!" Aiden seethes.

"You are owed nothing," Will snaps.

I place a hand on his arm, look to Aiden and ask, "Magic? Well, aside from murdering me, how can you restore your magic?"

Aiden looks me up and down with a sinister grin on his face, he is keeping his temper in check for the time being. "There must be a sacrifice," Aiden shrugs. "There is no other way."

My stomach drops. "So, I have to die. That's the only way?" My voice is barely audible over the storm. "I have to die?"

"Well, not you specifically. The world does not in fact revolve around you, darling," Aiden says flippantly, cleaning his nails with that wicked dagger. "There are some requirements for the sacrifice though," he looks at me as he says it.

I can feel my temper flaring now. "What kind of requirements, Aiden?"

"Well, so far, the ritual only seems to work when a girl is used. A beautiful, young, spirited girl."

Aiden takes a step toward me, leaving Cash a bit less guarded. Aiden's eyes are on mine, intent and glowing through the darkness. Beside me, Will's chin dips in an almost imperceptible nod. One of the crew members across the circle begins to inch closer to Cash. Will pinches the soft flesh of my arm.

"How do you know that?"

I have to keep Aiden talking, I have to keep him distracted while Will plays out the plan he has come up with. But part of me wants, no, needs to know the answers to these questions too. "How do you know that those are the requirements?"

"Why, I've tested it of course," Aiden smiles. Oh, he does love talking about himself, especially if it is about his *cleverness.*

"Who did you test it on?" I ask, and my shock is not an act when he replies.

"I have tested it many times. Girls, boys, younger, older. I have tried it all over the years."

He takes another step, and so does the pirate across the circle. The man is almost to Cash now.

"How many?" I ask, my teeth grinding together. "How many people have you killed?"

Aiden's eyes flash and lightning strikes, illuminating his features: the wide, sinister grin. "Countless. All for the greater good, of course."

"The greater good?" I can feel the fire building inside of me. "You're delusional, insane. You're a sadistic killer!" I shout.

Anger fills Aiden's eyes, but a quiet sob drags his attention from me. Cash is now standing behind a line of pirates, all ready, swords and daggers drawn. Miles is at the front of them all. A deadly wall of steel and men. Aiden whirls on me and Will, teeth bared and wicked dagger angled. But Will is ready too. His sword is pointed directly at Aiden's throat, and he is angling himself in front of me.

"Bested again, brother," Will smiles, cocking his head to the side. "Perhaps your obsession with pretty things has proven to be your weakness."

"You bastard," Aiden spits. Then his gaze is on me. "You little bitch!"

"You may call me whatever you'd like, but you will not speak to her that way." Will twists his arm, pushing the tip of his sword closer to Aiden's throat.

Aiden's eyes flash, the stones in his crown pulsing with them. Then lightning strikes the main mast. Splinters shower over us, the cracking of the wood louder than the thunder that follows. But Will does not so much as flinch. I, on the other hand, can't hold my scream in, and cover my head, sure that history is about to repeat itself and the Jolly Roger will end up destroyed once more.

The ship rocks violently as the waves get bigger, rougher. Sea water spills onto the deck, washing over my boots and soaking my feet inside. Aiden's face changes into something I have not seen from him before. Uncertainty, hesitation. I almost laugh. I don't think that he has ever once doubted himself, not even for a moment. Though the look fades quickly, replaced by the typical coy, smug look he usually wears, it will remain forever in my mind. As satisfying as it was to see Aiden doubt his cleverness, I know that it will only fuel his rage, potentially at our peril.

"This is far from over," Aiden flicks his gaze around the circle. "Good luck getting off the island this time," he adds with a wink in my direction. Then he pushes off the deck and shoots into the stormy sky.

CHAPTER 6

The storm continues to rage even after Aiden is far out of sight. The crew waits for a few minutes before releasing a collective breath. It was smart of them to wait just in case Aiden decided to double back for round two, but I think he was humiliated enough to keep away, at least for a little while. Once the crew has dispersed, Will silently signals to Miles to get Cash inside. When I start to follow them, eager to escape the cold rain, Will holds me back.

"Are you alright, love?" he asks, pushing a soaked lock of hair from my eyes.

Too quickly, I nod, "I'm fine."

Will doesn't notice it. He only looks me up and down before pulling me into his embrace, seemingly satisfied by my physical state.

"What are we going to do about the boy?" he asks.

"I suppose that depends on which boy you're referring to," I shrug.

He huffs a little laugh. "I was referring to the one now aboard my ship, but I suppose both."

I wrap my arms around his waist, pulling him close to my body. Shivering, I press myself against him as rain drips from my nose onto my lips.

"I have to check on Cash, make sure he's alright," I say into his chest.

Will feels warm, despite being soaking wet, and I absorb all the warmth that I can. He stiffens slightly at my words, but returns the embrace, chin resting on the top of my head.

"Of course," he sighs.

I pull back enough to look him in the eyes. "As for your brother, I am going to kill that bastard once and for all."

Will's eyes turn as stormy as the sky above us, steel grey instead of the usual brilliant blue. A muscle in

his jaw twitches.

From the second that I found out Aiden was still alive, the anger inside of me started to grow, but when I saw Cash on the deck, when I saw how badly he had been hurt...well, I have never felt that level of rage before. Aiden cannot go undefeated any longer; he has to pay for the things he has done.

"I know he's your brother, Will. But he is *evil*. There is no other way," I say. "He would kill every last one of us if it meant he would get his powers back."

Will steps back, hand rising to scrub at his face. "I know. I just wish there were another way."

I pull him back in, stretching up onto my frozen toes to kiss him lightly on the lips. "I do too," I assure him. "And if we somehow figure out another way, then we will take that path instead."

He stares hard into my eyes for a moment longer before sighing again. "Shall we go tend to your friend, then?"

As happy as I am to dry off and change, I am not entirely ready to face Cash. The way he looked at me on the deck...it was so cold, it chilled me more than the weather did. Even worse, I don't blame him one bit. I deserve the hate he feels for me; it's my fault that he is in this situation at all. Will takes my hand and together we head inside. The candles and lamps in the room are all lit, radiating a small amount of much needed heat into the small room that serves as the captain's quarters.

Cash is seated in Will's chair behind the desk, a blanket wrapped around his shoulders. It hides most of the wounds and blood, but it doesn't hide the bruises on his face. It doesn't hide the cut above his right eyebrow, or the partially dried blood at the corner of his mouth. My chest is so tight I can barely breathe. I hurry to the desk, crouching beside the large wooden chair.

"Are you alright?" I ask, moving to place a hand on his arm. He jerks away from me and I snatch my hand back like it was burned.

Cash does not look at me when he says, "No, actually, I am not alright."

"Cash-" I start, but he cuts me off.

"Don't! Just don't Elena. All I want is to get the hell out of wherever we are and go home."

My mouth opens, then snaps shut. How am I supposed to tell him that we are in Neverland? That he can't go home? Will steps up behind me then, the pirate persona back in full force.

"I'm afraid you won't be leaving anytime soon, lad," he says, unbuckling his sword belt and tossing it onto the desk.

Cash glares at Will. "I knew there was something off about you. You think you're a pirate or something?"

"Aye," Will says. "I am a pirate. Problem mate?"

I watch as Cash takes in Will's appearance. The fitted black pants and the loose white shirt tucked into them. The heavy black boots on his feet, the long, dark coat adorned with large brass buttons. Finally, his eyes land on the hook that replaces Will's missing hand.

"Is this some kind of joke?" Cash bursts into laughter. "You're insane, certified crazy."

All hints of amusement leave Will's face then. "I would watch my tongue if I were you, boy." "This is ridiculous!" Cash shouts. "Just let me go, I want to go home!"

"You can't, Cash. We're going to do everything we can to get home, but you can't leave right now." My voice is thick with emotion and held back tears.

"Why the hell not?" Cash demands.

I turn my head to the side, squeeze my eyes shut against the flood threatening to spill out.

"Because boy," Will steps in. "you are in Neverland. Your only option at the moment is to remain a guest on my ship; unless you would prefer to return to the island to take your chances with my brother?"

When I open my eyes, Cash's face is white as bone. He stares hard at Will, then me, then looks away, jaw clenched. Will smirks before turning away and stripping off his wet shirt. I study Cash's face, willing him to look at me, just for a moment. He only stares into the flame of one of the candles on the desk.

Will returns with dry clothes for me and for Cash. I raise my eyebrows at him, a silent plea to let me speak to Cash alone. Thankfully, Will knows me well and understands my unspoken request. Even though he does not look very happy about it, he simply brushes a kiss across my lips before striding out of the cabin, head held high.

I toss Cash's fresh clothes onto the desk and retreat backwards with my own. Turning on my heel, I go into the small bathing chamber and change quickly. Too quickly. Because when I return, Cash is standing with his shirt only half on. I can't help but stare at the bruises of varying size and color that cover his body, along with the deep, criss-crossing gashes. Those will more than likely scar, serving as a constant reminder of me and the pain he experienced because of me. His eyes meet mine and I look away quickly, but he knows I was staring. Quickly, he buttons the shirt before resuming his seat behind the desk.

"I'm sorry," I say quietly. "You wouldn't be here if it weren't for me."

"I don't know what you expect me to say, Elena," his voice is flat, dead.

"Something," I am whispering now. "Anything."

His eyes are cold when they flick up to mine. "I wish I had never met you."

I stop breathing. The pressure in my chest is unbearable. "Oh."

It's the only thing I can think of to say. Anger starts to weave in with the initial hurt that his words caused. I understand that he's lashing out because he's hurting and scared, but to say he wishes he had never met me...he took it too far.

I see it, the moment Cash realizes how much of an effect his words had on me. His features soften just slightly. For a second, when he opens his mouth, I think he is going to say something, but then he closes it and says nothing more.

"I'm sorry for what happened to you, I truly am, but I will not stand here and let you use me as your personal punching bag," I say as calmly as I can manage before willing my features into neutrality. I don't wait to see if he responds. Instead, I straighten my spine, turn and walk out the door without looking back. Only when the heavy door closes behind me do I exhale, one long, shaky breath. Then I pull myself together and go to join Will and the rest of the crew. Cash is safe, Aiden has been subdued, for now. All I can do now is help us all get home. If Cash wants to hate me forever, then that's on him.

ill waits for Elena to arrive in the crowded galley. A plate of food sits untouched on the table before him. It has not been long, but it feels like an eternity. When she finally walks through the door, he can see it instantly, the pain and the anger in her eyes. She stalks over and sits down beside him on the wooden bench. He can practically feel the fire burning inside her.

"I'm fine," she insists. He knows she is not. Whatever happened in that room, whatever that boy said to her, it hurt her. Will would love nothing more than to pummel the boy for hurting her, but Elena would not want that. Perhaps he can convince the little sod to spar with him and teach him a lesson that way...she likely would not approve of that either though. Of course, his soft-hearted Elena feels that all of this is her fault, when really, it is his fault.

It is his fault for ever coming into her life in the first place. Will knows, deep down, that he should have stayed in Neverland and not gone to London after her. He should have let the darkness and the wine consume him and left her to be happy with the blond boy, or someone more deserving of her. He is not good for her, and he is not good enough for her, but she loves him anyway, and he will never understand why.

Aiden stumbles into his treehouse soaking wet and freezing. Keeping the storm going is exhausting now. He is using up so much of his depleted magic that he could not even summon enough to keep himself dry. Just flying makes him tired. He should stop the storm, but no, he is far too petty for that. This is personal, and he will drain himself to his limits if it will deprive his enemies of any reprieve.

How dare they trick him and steal his fun away! How dare they speak to him like he is a stupid child! They will pay. He will make them pay. He will strip them of every shred of happiness before he kills them. And their deaths, those will not be quick, and certainly not painless. No. Their deaths will be poetic.

Cash takes his time before joining us in the galley. The room goes silent the second he walks in. Cash does not make eye contact with anyone as he walks between the tables and slides onto the bench, a healthy distance away from Will and me. I don't blame him. I can only imagine what the crew thinks of the whole situation. We show up unannounced with Will barking orders and warnings of an attack, and then Aiden shows up with a guy they've never seen before and they are expected to rescue and protect him. Then of course, there is the thick tension surrounding Cash, Will, and me. I can only hope that pirates are above gossip, but from the hushed whispers and not so sly looks being exchanged, I am probably hoping in vain.

Cash finally looks around, eyeing everyone and everything before piling a plate up with food and devouring it all before I am even halfway through my own meal. He fills his plate once more, piling it high with bread and meat. My chest tightens. Not only did Aiden torture him, he starved him. Aiden couldn't have taken Cash more than a day or so ago; although, considering the way time moves here in Neverland, Cash has likely been here for at least a few days, likely closer to a week. Despite the anger I feel at how he treated me, I can't suppress the shudder that ripples through me as I think about just how much Cash has likely endured so far in Neverland.

Shoving his empty plate away, Cash looks to Will. "I'm exhausted," he says. "Where will I be sleeping?"

Will arches one eyebrow at me from across the table. I

just shrug. This is his ship; he can give the instructions. Will looks to Miles and gives a nod.

Miles rises and says, "Follow me, boy." His voice is so deep that it echoes through the galley.

Cash scrambles to his feet without another word and rushes out the door on Miles's heels.

The room instantly erupts into hushed murmurs. Will only rolls his eyes and finishes the food on his own plate. "Your friend will be sleeping with the crew during his stay," he says between bites. "He'll be fine," he adds when I raise my eyebrows at him. "The men are harmless."

"Harmless!" I choke on the word, as well as my food. "Will, I've seen them fight. The men on this ship are far from harmless."

Will only shrugs, "Fair point, love." He props an elbow on the table, chin resting on the palm of his good hand, and cocks one eyebrow at me. "But what about me?" His voice is rough and low, his eyes burning into mine. "Am I harmless?"

My breath hitches and my palms go slick with sweat. How is it possible that this man can do so much to me with just a look and a few well thought out words?

"You," I reply in a hushed voice. "Are quite possibly the most dangerous thing in Neverland."

Will's eyes sparkle with amusement. A grin stretches across his face.

"Is that right?" he teases.

I mirror his stance, elbow on the table, chin in hand, and do my best to imitate his seductive voice. "Yes," I say. "Because you are lethal in battle. And also because you're charming. No, you are dazzling. You make my heart race."

Now he just looks cocky. The bastard. But God, do I love him. I curl my lips into a smirk. "The primary reason you are the most dangerous though," I lower my voice further. "Is because of what you do to me. To my heart. To my body."

Our eyes are locked, Will's are wide, full of desire. I press my lips together, trying to stifle the smile at his reaction. Will continues to stare at me for a minute longer, his eyes burning like blue fire, searching my face. Suddenly he stands.

"Rest while you can men," he addresses the crew still present. "And leave the boy be." There is a command in his voice that I know the crew would be foolish to disobey.

"Elena," Will saunters around the table to offer me his hand. "We should get some rest as well," he says, but his eyes are full of mischief. For some reason, I highly doubt that we will get much rest tonight.

A while later, Will is drawing small circles on my back with his fingers while I doze on his chest.

"Elena," his voice rumbles through his chest, rousing me.

"Hmm?" I sigh.

"Suppose we do survive this, and we make it back to London. What then?" he asks quietly.

Pushing up onto my elbows, I stare hard into his eyes. "What do you mean?"

Anxiety causes my chest to tighten. Is this his way of telling me that he doesn't want to come back with me? He has seemed so much happier and more himself since we arrived back in Neverland, maybe he wants to stay. "What I'm wondering," his voice interrupts my thoughts. "Is what does our future look like in your mind?"

"Oh," my anxiety subsides a bit. "Well…"

What do I see for our future? Resting my chin on my hand, I allow myself to imagine what our lives might look like down the road. I'm still so young, I don't even know what I want to do yet. A few different scenarios run through my mind, but in each one, there is one constant. Will. I can't picture any future without him in it.

"Will," I begin. "I don't have the slightest idea what our future holds."

His breathing stops, I can hear his heartrate jump. Turning my head, I reach out a hand and place it on his cheek.

"I may not know exactly what our future looks like, but one thing I'm sure of is that it will be *our* future."

He meets my eyes then; I imagine that the anxiety in them is a mirror image of my own.

"I don't see any kind of future without you. I just want you, and I want us to be happy."

Will's eyes are shining with tears. Pulling me on top of him, he crushes his mouth to mine. His lips travel across my jaw to my ear.

"I love you," he whispers before placing his hand on the back of my neck and guiding my lips back to his. "I will get you home, I swear it," he says between kisses.

Just like that, I am lost in him. I will never be able to explain the effect that Will has on me, or how just a simple touch or a few words from him can intoxicate me so easily, but it happens more often than I'd like to admit.

Elena's words echo through Cash's skull as he stares at the wood planks of the ceiling above him. He knows it was wrong to take his emotions out on her, after all, it's not entirely her fault that he's in this situation. The hammock assigned to him sways gently with the rocking of the ship but does nothing to calm him or lull him to sleep.

A pirate ship—he is on a bloody pirate ship. As stunning as it is, all dark, shiny wood, and intricate details, he wonders how he managed to end up in some sort of twisted fairytale. Every boy plays pirate as a child, so in a way it should be a dream come true. But Cash feels as though he has been sucked into a nightmare instead. He wonders if his mother knows that he is missing; he wonders what his friends think of his absence. What is he going to tell them when he returns? If he returns...

How will he explain the many wounds on his body? Wounds that are surely going to scar, wounds inflicted during hours of torture in that cave. Cash shudders at the thought. The image of the sadistic look on his captor's face is burned into his memory forever. He can remember the sting of the dagger as the boy dragged it down his torso while Cash hung by his wrists. Cash's injuries are not quite as painful now that he had a chance to clean them. He hopes that the scarring will be minimal, but there are several rather deep cuts that likely won't heal perfectly.

The events that have occurred have certainly changed Cash's life. He will never forget them. Every time he takes off his shirt he will be reminded of that cave, of this ship. Cash doesn't know what else might happen to him during his time in this awful place, hopefully nothing worth remembering, but if living the rest of his life with bad memories means that he makes it home alive, then it is a price he is willing to pay.

The fairy hovers outside the boy's little house. He used too much magic today; now he is weak, vulnerable. She can see him shaking even from her station outside. The boy refused the fairy's offer of help. He is *always* dismissing her...and yet, she would do anything for him. She cannot stay away from him. And so, she hovers outside of his window, worrying and watching over him from afar.

Will looks down at the girl dozing beside him. He had thought that he never wanted to step foot in Neverland again, but being back has lifted his mood greatly. Being back on his ship, close to the sea, around his closest companions, it is much more natural to him than living in Elena's world. Part of him does want to remain in Neverland, but after what she said about their future, he knows he could never ask her to stay. He must get her back to London and he must do everything he can to give her the life she deserves.

The knowledge that his brother is alive is both a blessing and a curse. On the one hand, he is happy that the girl he loves is not responsible for Aiden's death. He knows that it weighed heavily on her mind, as well as his own. Despite her insistence that she be the one to kill Aiden, Will does not want that for Elena. She is holding onto a lot of anger, which is understandable considering all she has been through. Murder is not something Will would like to see added to that list though. It would be something she would never be able to let go of. She has enough bad memories to carry throughout her life.

No, if Aiden has to die, it must be Will that kills him. He hopes with every ounce of his being that it does not come to that. If there is any way to spare his brother and, hopefully, render him harmless at the same time, then he will do anything he possibly can to take that path. But Elena's life, her safety, that is the most important thing to Will. If any harm should come to her, he will do what he must to avenge her.

Will can feel the darkness trying to shove its way back into his heart. He shakes his head. No, the darkness was expelled from him, these dark thoughts are entirely his own, and one of the many reasons he is not good for Elena. He should not be thinking about murder, especially murdering his own brother. But what choice does he really have? Will is trapped in a situation where there will only be loss. He will either lose Elena, or he will lose his brother. In a way though, didn't he already lose his brother long ago?

The boy who rules over Neverland is not the same boy who came to this place so many years ago. Power has corrupted him, turned his soul dark, made him into a madman and a murderer. And so, Will must do whatever it takes.

~

Inside of his tiny home, the boy rages. Shattered trinkets litter the furs on the floor. He slams his shaking fist down onto a hand mirror lying on the table. It cracks and splinters; smears of his blood coat the glass. The boy summons his magic to heal the slices criss-crossing his hand. Nothing happens. The storm began to dissipate not long ago as exhaustion set in causing his magic to fail.

Picking up the shattered mirror, Aiden hurls it with all his might. It crashes through the window, leaving shards of glass in its wake. Outside, a child begins to cry, but Aiden cannot bring himself to care. They humiliated him. Elena and the damned pirates made a mockery of him and he will not tolerate it. They stole his plaything; they threw his diminished magic in his face. It is unacceptable.

Another wave of rage crashes through him and he is lost to the sound of shattered treasures.

CHAPTER 7

My eyes flutter open; the smell of the sea fills my nose. Will is curled around my body, chest to my back, one arm draped over my torso. The warmth of his breath tickles my ear. The urge to stretch my limbs is there, but I do not want to disturb Will. Might as well soak up the peace while we can. It will not last long; peace never lasts here in Neverland. Not with Aiden wreaking havoc constantly.

My mind wanders, and then I am thinking of Aiden. He looks so much different from the first time I saw him. I remember thinking he was so angelic looking. Those eyes, both startling and beautiful. The strong jawline and the slightly crooked smile, his straight, proportional nose. How could such an attractive person be so rotten inside? If I could see his soul, I imagine that it would be black, empty of anything other than hate and a thirst for more power. And yet, in a way, I do pity that beautiful boy. It can't be pleasant, living with so much darkness inside. Behind me, Will begins to stir and I force all thoughts of his brother out of my head. He pulls me tightly against him, nuzzling my neck and sending chills through my body.

"Well," he purrs. "Good morning."

Heat pools in my core. "Good morning."

A smile tugs at the corners of my lips as I try to turn over and face him. Will pins me against him though, apparently perfectly content with our positioning. Will hasn't been affectionate like this since leaving Neverland. It's like he allowed the reality of living in the real world to affect him so negatively that he couldn't focus on any of the good things. It is yet another reminder of all that he gave up to be with me, and it makes me sad. Wiggling out of his grasp, I roll onto my back. Will slides across the sheets to my side.

"Don't spoil my fun," he murmurs into my hair as the fingers of his good hand trail up my thigh, over my hip, up my arm.

· · ·

S parks zing through my veins.
"Will," his name sounds like a prayer on my lips.
But I am not in the mood; my thoughts brought a heavy cloud of anxiety and doubt over my head.

"I do love the way you say my name," he says, his voice as rough as a gravel road.

"W ill," I say again, but this time there is a hint of warning in it. "Shouldn't we get up?"
What I'm really thinking though, is if dragging Will back to London with me is the right thing to do. I just want him to be happy, and he seems so much happier here.
Will sighs deeply.

"I 'd rather not," he grumbles. "But if you insist. He nips at my ear, sending fresh waves of electricity through my body. Rolling onto his back, he begins to rise.

"W hat are we going to do about Aiden?" I ask hesitantly.

W ill, in the process of pulling his clothes on, goes absolutely rigid and sinks back onto the bed. I regret bringing it up, I know it's hard for him, but we need a plan, a *good* plan, if we are all going to survive. My anger has subsided some. The desire to plunge a dagger into Aiden's heart is still there, but an uneasiness at the thought of actually doing it has crept in too. Do I really want to be a murderer?

"I don't know, love," Will finally says. "I honestly do not know."

My heart sinks at his answer. I was hoping that he might have thought of something, anything, that could get us out without any loss of life.

"We'll figure it out," I try to sound reassuring, but there is no confidence in my voice. Will only nods and pushes himself off the bed.

The process of bathing and dressing goes quietly, both of us lost in our own thoughts. His are most likely centered around his brother, around the inevitable carnage to come, and what he can do to prevent the potentially catastrophic events that will occur before we escape Neverland again. *If* we escape. My thoughts, well, those are a bit more complicated...

I fell for Will almost instantly, and since then, I've only really doubted my feelings for him once. I'm not doubting my feelings for him now, but being in Neverland with Will, and Cash, and Aiden...it's definitely getting to me. How stupid of me to get involved with so many guys. If I were smarter, I wouldn't have gotten involved with anyone. Then again, considering the fact that Aiden used his manipulative magic to lure me here in the first place, I didn't have much of a choice with that one. Will snuck up on me in a way. When I opened my eyes on this ship for the first time, I wasn't expecting to fall in love with its captain. I did fall though, and no matter what happens to us, I don't think I could ever regret it. Then there's Cash. Being with Cash would be simple, easy, normal. There would be no worries of murderous boys trying to kill me, no worries about manipulative fairies, or dangerous pirates. If I had refused Aiden and never come to Neverland, I would probably be in my dorm room, studying for exams, living a normal teenage existence with the sweet boy who bought me a Christmas tree ornament on our first date.

Will snakes his arms around me from behind, making me jump. He pulls back.

"Are you alright, love?" he leans around to look at my face.

I nod quickly. "I'm fine, just thinking. You startled me is all."

. . .

Will gently takes me by the shoulders, turning me until I was facing him. "Elena," he says quietly. "It will be alright. We will survive this."

I almost believe him, but the fact that he can't look me in the eyes as he says that last sentence sows doubt through my mind. I let him hug me tight and whisper reassuring words in my ear, all the while imagining all the ways things could go wrong, and all the ways my life would be different if I had never come here in the first place.

It appears that the storm has let up, for the time being at least. We emerge into the watery, midmorning sunlight to find the crew hard at work, Cash alongside them. Miles is showing him how to adjust the rigging and the sails. Both Cash and his mentor are shirtless. I look away quickly, but not before I catch sight of Cash's injuries in the light. They do look a little better, but far from healed.

"I'm just going to check in with the crew," Will says, brushing a kiss lightly over the back of my hand.

. . .

I nod, heading down to the galley by myself. Upon entering, I find that I am the only one in the room and take full advantage of it. I stuff bread, fruit and cheese into my mouth while I attempt to sort through my thoughts and emotions. By the time I'm finished eating, Will has still not made an appearance. Instead of waiting for him, I head back to the deck to find out what is keeping him. My intentions are to train today. I had been doing so well while I was here before, and now I fear that I am severely out of shape. Not to mention that I need to practice with the weapons, considering I haven't so much as seen a sword in weeks.

The sound of clashing swords rings through the air. I reach the top deck to find Will and Cash, surrounded by the crew, going at each other. Will is now also shirtless, and I can't help but appreciate the way his muscles move beneath his tan skin. The crew is watching them intently, laughing and cheering them on. It seems that Will has taken it upon himself to train Cash. Or to show off and intimidate him, I'm not entirely sure which. Though, knowing Will, it's most likely a bit of both.

As I get closer, I can see the sheen of sweat coating both of their chests. Their skin glistens in the hazy sunlight filtering through the clouds. Averting my eyes, I square my shoulders and step into the circle of pirates. They part to let me through. Will gives me a wink and a grin before striking out at Cash with the sword in his hand. Cash doesn't take his eyes off of Will. Each time their weapons collide, I see Cash wince, but he doesn't back down. The fact that he's training at all is surprising considering the extent of his injuries. Up close, I'm able to get a better look at the gashes on his torso. They look awfully painful. Some are so deep that I am amazed they haven't split open again. Others are thin and already look to be fading. The bruises on his face and chest are various shades of purple, black and yellow. I am honestly amazed that he's alive.

Will strikes at Cash over and over, their swords connecting loudly. He shows off his excellent footwork by twirling and spinning in between strikes. Cash grits his teeth against the pain he is surely experiencing; sweat is now pouring down his face. Still, he does not back down. Shifting my weight from one foot to the other, I wait for them to finish, eager to get in on the action myself. I can't help but wonder how this sparring session will end though. Most likely in injury, but hopefully they will just wear each other out.

After a few more jabs at each other, and a bit of swearing, they finally call it quits. Cash's face splits into a smile despite being disheveled and sweaty. Will actually smiles back. "There may be hope for you yet, boy," he says approvingly.

Cash grins. "And you're not so bad, for a pirate."

"Ahem," I clear my throat loudly. I'm anxious to see

how much of my training I actually retained. I also have a bit of pent-up anger to get out and training sounds like the best way to do so. Will looks to me instantly, and to my surprise, so does Cash.

"Ready for a turn, love?" Will asks, mischief both on his face and in his voice.

Cash's eyes go wide. "You let her fight?"

My eyes narrow. "He doesn't *let* me do anything."

Will chuckles. "She is right about that. Elena does as she pleases."

"And I deserve to know how to protect myself just as much as you," I add with a level look in Cash's direction. I haven't forgotten his words from last night, the sting of them is still there.

"Fair enough," Cash nods.

He holds out the sword he had been practicing with. I

smile but wave him off and pull a small sword from the loop in my pants. Will nods with approval when he realizes that I haven't forgotten his rule about never being unarmed. He flips his sword into the air, catching it deftly in his one good hand.

"Show off," I mutter.

He laughs again and lunges for me. I parry the strike and slash a little too wildly. He twists out of my path, knocking me off balance and sending me stumbling across the deck.

"Focus Elena," Will says quietly.

He takes a step back, allowing me to right myself and gather my wits. I take a deep breath, but when I turn, I catch sight of the smug look on Cash's face. Anger begins to simmer deep inside of me. "Again," I say through clenched teeth. Will comes at me again, but this time I am ready for it. I spin away from his attack, launching my own against him. Stabbing, deflecting, slashing, I push him back until his back is against the wheel and the tip of my sword is at his throat.

· · ·

"Good form, love. Well done," Will grins, batting my blade away and pressing a quick kiss to my sweaty forehead.

I can't resist giving Cash a smug smile of my own before stalking off to change into a fresh set of clothes. Will saunters into the room just as I am buttoning the last button of my shirt. He wipes his face on the fabric of his own discarded shirt that he carries in his hand. His bare chest is still slick with sweat.

"You did well," he compliments me. "Your friend did well also, much to my surprise."

"Cash isn't exactly my friend," I say quietly. I sort of expect Will to be angry, but instead he crosses the room to me, folding me into his arms.

"Give him time, Elena," he says into my hair. I sigh, blinking against the tears threatening to fall from my eyes.

"He will come around. Think of what he's been through, what he is still going through," he adds.

. . .

"Exactly," I bury my face in his chest. "I wouldn't want to be friends with the girl who got me kidnapped and tortured."

"Just give it time," Will repeats.

He squeezes me so tightly, it's as if he is trying to hold all my broken pieces together. Closing my eyes, I breathe in his comforting scent and pretend that it's working.

The King of Neverland is gathering his troops. He looks over the clearing filled with lost children and fairies. They all stare up at him, waiting. The boy clears his throat.

"It is time. Time to rid Neverland of the pirates, time to reclaim what is ours!" His voice rings out across the clearing, loud and clear. "Are you with me?"

Whoops and cheers fill the air, echoing off the canopy of green above. Many of them will perish, but that is a sacrifice that the boy is willing to make. He smiles that feral smile and rallies what little magic he has left to him. It is time for war.

~

The fairy stares up at the boy from her place amongst the crowd. He did not allow her to be by his side for this. No matter, she knows that she will be fighting with him when the time comes. The fairy also knows that her life may end during this battle. If she dies protecting him though, then it is a sacrifice she is willing to make.

The boy's eyes flare and he smiles that beautiful, terrifying smile. No, the fairy would not mind dying for him at all.

~

Back on deck, Cash and the crew are still training with swords and daggers. Probably for the best. When the time comes, I can't be worrying about Cash. I already have Will to worry about. If I allow myself to be distracted, it could be the end of me.

Will and I watch the sparring from a distance before he silently beckons for me to follow him. We walk to the opposite side of the ship. When we are far out of earshot, Will looks at me, wariness in those ocean eyes.

"As much as I hate to say this," he says, his words so quiet that the clashing of blades in the distance almost drowns them out. "It is time to call on the mermaids again."

I shudder. As much help as the mermaids were the last time around, they scare the hell out of me. I don't want to get anywhere near their sharp, needle-like teeth if I can avoid it.

"I never asked before," I say, just as quietly as he spoke. "But how do you summon the mermaids?"

Will gives me a half smile before reaching into the pocket of his coat. When he holds his hand out again, a battered coin lies in his palm. I've never seen it before, but it looks ancient, just like how you would think a piece of pirate treasure would look, so worn that I can't even tell if there were markings on it at some point. I give him a wry smile.

Will shrugs my look off, focusing now on the coin in his palm. He turns the coin twice, rubbing his thumb over the faded surface in a circular motion. All of the hair on my arms stands straight up as a ripple of energy shoots out around the ship. Will places the coin back into his pocket, patting it with his good hand.

"And now we wait," he says turning toward me.

I rub my hands up and down my arms. "What was that?"

. . .

"M agic," he laughs. "What else?"

I shrug before leaning over the railing to look down at the waves, arms still wrapped around myself. For a while, nothing happens.

"Where did you find that coin?" I ask Will. A piece of hair blows across my face prompting Will to reach out and push it behind my ear.

"I didn't find it. The mermaids gave it to me long ago to use if I ever needed to contact them."

"Oh," I suppose I was expecting a more climactic story behind the magic coin. Then a thought dawns on me. "But the mermaids don't exactly seem like the friendly, giving type, so why would they give you something like that?"

T urning to rest his elbows on the railing, Will gazes out at the sea, seemingly pondering his answer.

"I suppose," he begins. "That even though they are not fond of either of us, they decided that I was the lesser of two evils."

.   .   .

"You're not evil," I say moving to stand beside him.

"If you say so, love." Will smiles over at me, but it doesn't reach his eyes.

There is a flash of color beneath the ocean's surface and then the unearthly faces of the mermaids appear above the waves, smiling up at us with mouths full of needle teeth. Will greets them, speaks to them, explaining why we called on them, why we need their help once again. They stare up, horrifying smiles plastered on their beautiful faces as he pleads with them. When he finishes, one by one, they slowly disappear into the depths with a flick of jewel-colored tails.

The beautiful music of their language fills the air. All sounds of sparring and training and weapons ceases. Every man on the ship is now aware of the presence of the mermaids. I glance back. They are all frozen in place, weapons still in hand, listening to the mermaid's song.

"Will they help us?" I lean into Will's shoulder to whisper in his ear.

He shrugs. "They are deliberating."

. . .

"What is there to debate?" I can feel my temper spike. "They helped us before, why wouldn't they now?"

"Because," Will tilts his head toward mine. "If we lose, and my brother wins, there is no question that he will find a way to punish them." He states it so matter-of-factly.

I can feel the color drain from my face.

"Just stating facts, Elena," he turns his head to look into my eyes now. "We are up against an army of fairies and magic; the odds aren't exactly in our favor."

In a way it's comforting to know that Will trusts me enough not to sugarcoat it. He's being completely honest about our situation, which is both terrifying and oddly comforting.

"So, you have decided?" Will's voice brings me back to the present.

A shrill, high-pitched screeching fills the air. Their answer. "Very well," Will responds. And then the mermaids are gone with a flick of gem-colored tails.

. . .

"Well?" I demand.

"When the time comes, the mermaids will be here," Will says.

"That's a good thing, right?" The shaking in my hands has slowed.

"I hope so," Will shrugs. "They will stay close to the ship for the time being, my brother likely won't wait long to launch an attack against us.

My hands begin to shake, the trembling quickly spreading through my limbs. Not because I am afraid of the mermaids. But because it really just hit me that sometime soon, very soon, this ship will be a battleground, and there will be fatalities. I knew it was coming, but it feels too real now.

"Elena," Will reaches for me.

I step out of his grasp. Nausea hits me; my breakfast rises in my throat. I turn, sprinting across the deck to the captain's quarters where I barely make it to the bathing room before my stomach turns itself inside out.

Will is perched on the edge of his desk when I emerge, a pitcher of water beside him. Silently, he hands me a cup. I drink it down greedily. When I have drained the cup dry and set it on the desk, Will brushes his hand up my arm. But again, I step away. Tears well in my eyes.

"Not now, Will. It feels too much like a goodbye."

Will's face falls. "I'm not trying to scare you, Elena. But what if it is a goodbye? We don't know what may happen, and I want to soak you in while I can."

I can't stop the tears from flowing down my face. Hot and angry and fast. But this time, I let Will pull me in. I let him hold me while I fall to pieces in front of him. The thought of losing him, of watching him die, it's too much. My biggest fear isn't what could happen to me, but what could happen to Will, or Cash, or the crew. I wish that there was something I could do to prevent any violence or loss of life. Then again, if it comes down to it, would I have the strength to sacrifice my life if it meant saving everyone else's? I wish that I could say yes, but I'm not sure that would be true. Will has told me how strong I am, but in reality, I'm so weak.

. . .

I have to fight though; there isn't another option. So that's what I'll do, I will fight. I will fight hard until the very end, whether that end be mine, Will's, or Aiden's. With tooth, nail, and steel, I will fight. I let Will hold me tightly, his warmth seeping into me. I allow it to fuel the fire now burning brightly inside my chest. The fire he noticed the first time he met me, that Aiden noticed as he watched me from afar. The fire that brought me to Neverland. I never saw it in myself, but now, I can feel it. I will feed that fire now; I will let it rage and burn everything to ash if I must.

Cash's first experience with the mermaids was interesting, to say the least. Their song, language, whatever, was beautiful. He was told that they are very dangerous though, that he should steer clear of them. Apparently, Elena's pirate has enlisted them to aid in the battle that is to come. How lovely...

Cash doesn't have any desire to be part of a battle, but he most certainly doesn't want to die either. How has this become his life? How did he end up in this situation? Training with swords and fighting side by side with pirates just to stay alive, it's absurd. If it weren't for the wounds all over his body, Cash might still think this all an elaborate dream. But this is his life, and Cash is hellbent on surviving, so he will fight. He won't do it for Elena, or for Will and his band of pirates, but for himself. To survive.

Will holds Elena close. He will keep her as close to him as he can until the end. Whether it be his end, or his brother's, or hers. But oh, how he hopes it will not be her end. He wouldn't be able to handle seeing her die. Seeing her battered and bloody and broken the last time was far too much for him to take. Will wonders, if push comes to shove, will he truly be able to kill his brother?

Will knows that no matter the cost, he will fight, even if that price is his own life. He will fight for her, for them. He will fight for their future together, if there is one. And if there is not, he will fight for her future without him. If he should fall during the battle, he hopes that his efforts and his death will not be for nothing.

The boy hovers just off the coast of his island. The children move so *slowly!* It would be so easy to just sprinkle them all with fairy dust, but an airborne army of that size would be far too noticeable. No, they must travel by boat, while he and the fairies take to the skies.

It will not be a quick fight, nor will it be easy an easy one, but he *will* destroy the pirates, he will destroy his brother, and he will take what is rightfully his. Elena, and in turn, his power. And so the boy hovers, and waits, and plans.

~

The fairy ushers the children along and into the boats lined up along the beach. Aiden was kind enough to leave the younger children behind with a small host of fairies. No child under the age of ten was permitted to come along. This may be war, but the beautiful, terrible boy does have a heart.

The fairy is hopeful that most of the children going into battle will not come to harm. She quite likes most of them, as much as a fairy can like a human at least. They are rather entertaining. But the boy...oh, that would be the real tragedy. If Aiden falls, then it will all be over for Tatiana. Her heart would be broken, her king would be dead, and the pirates and the girl would most likely not let her live after her betrayal.

Maybe, just maybe, if she protects him, if she helps the boy win his war, he will finally see her worth and realize that he needs her. That he *wants* her. And so, the fairy ushers the last of the children onto the boat and begins the journey across the Never Sea, towards the final battle.

CHAPTER 8

The mermaids proved their worth as allies quickly when they brought the news that a host of boats was heading for the Jolly Roger. Boats filled with the Lost Children. I hadn't thought that was a possibility. I underestimated Aiden; I had assumed he wasn't that horrible. Of course, however, he is. It's not enough for him to bring the fairies with him, to sacrifice their lives for his own selfish cause. No, of course he would bring the children along too. Part of me wonders if it is to distract us, for he surely knows that I will not let any harm come to a bunch of kids.

Dinner is nothing but a war council. Will, Miles and the rest of the crew have spent the past hour discussing strategy. Will wants to have a solid plan of what moves they should make and when, as well as which weapons to bring out and when. Miles's suggestion had been to use the mermaids to sink the boats before they could ever reach the Jolly Roger. I had to interject at that point, something that Will was not entirely thrilled with. But I could not sit there and let them decide to leave dozens of innocent children to drown.

Most of the crew argued that the Lost Children are not innocent, seeing as they are on their way here at this very moment to go to war with us. Against that, I argued that they don't know any better than what Aiden tells them to do. In the end, Will sided with me, agreeing that we can't just kill them. I also talked him into giving orders to capture them upon their arrival on the ship. I got plenty of sideways looks from the crew for that. Will did make it clear to me that if they came at any of the pirates with the intent to kill though, that the pirates were at full liberty to defend themselves. I know that Will is trying to find a middle ground, so I don't argue anymore.

I think it helped that Cash actually backed me in the discussion. At first I was a little shocked that he even wanted to be part of the meeting, but Will pointed out that Cash's life is on the line as well, and he will be fighting just like the rest of us, so really he *should* be a part of it. Cash didn't say much throughout the discussions, that is, until the kids were brought up. It surprised me when he finally spoke and backed me up, arguing fiercely against any plan that would end with dozens of dead kids. Maybe he wasn't so much trying to back me up, maybe it just boiled down to his morals and mine being similar, and neither of us being able to stand seeing the Lost Children die for no reason.

In the end, this is how everything was decided: the mermaids will do their best to deter the boats from getting close enough to board the ship. They will disable the boats without harming the children, and then drag the disabled boats back to the island to keep the children away from the battle. The guns and cannons will be used to keep the airborne force consisting of Aiden and his fairies at bay. There will still be hand to hand combat; there is no avoiding it. Fairies will get through and fight alongside Aiden. We have plenty of weapons, enough swords, daggers, and pistols to go around. But they have one thing we don't: magic. And that is a very good weapon to have, since we don't have any defenses against it.

Once the last of the details are as hammered out as they can be, Will shakes the hand of his first mate, and the hand of every other man in the room, including Cash, before everyone goes their separate ways. The crew splits up, some going to prepare weapons, some to keep watch, and the remaining to rest. They will rotate in groups, resting in shifts until it is time.

Will and I retire to our quarters, but we do not sleep for a very long while. We spend what could possibly be our last night together soaking in every second of each other's presence. For hours, all I know is his skin on mine, his hands in my hair, and his lips. He says my name over and over between kisses. He whispers it, growls it. All the while I am silently praying to any deity that will listen that this man will survive the coming battle.

Cash sits through the meeting at dinner mostly silently. He picks at the food on his plate without eating much, and he listens. The wounds on his body sting and ache, and all of his muscles are sore from training for hours. It was quite thrilling, the training. Cash was surprised they let him do so at all, but Elena's pirate, Will, had insisted that he know how to properly use a sword and defend himself.

Cash's childhood fantasy of being a pirate has come true, and while it is exciting, it is also terrifying. Soon he is going to be part of a real battle, and there is a solid chance that he could die. He does his best to shove the morbid thoughts away but being surrounded by pirates all talking strategy and weapons makes it impossible.

When the first mate suggests letting the mermaids rip apart the boats, Cash had to interject, though he was relieved that Elena spoke up against the idea first. He may get on well with the crew, but that could have changed if they were put off by him questioning their tactics. It is much easier for him to just agree with Elena. He has yet to see any of the kids on the island, but he knows he cannot let the pirates slaughter them just because they are following Aiden's orders. They are just kids, kids who have basically been raised by a psychopath; they don't know any better.

When the pirates disperse, Cash goes below deck to his hammock and tries to close his eyes, but sleep does not come. He lies awake most of the night knowing that tomorrow he could die, and praying that he makes it out alive.

M y eyes snap open to the sound of a loud and incessant bell ringing somewhere in the distance. Dim, pre-dawn light filters around the thick curtains covering the floor to ceiling windows behind Will's desk. "Will?" my voice is still thick with sleep. I reach my hand across the mattress, feeling for him, but my fingers graze nothing but cool sheets. Then he is there, shaking me awake.

"Elena, get up!" The panic in his voice sets my heart pounding.

"It's time?" I ask. My voice only cracks a little.

"Aye," he says, practically pulling me out of bed now. "It is time."

His eyes are so bright in the dimness; there is a wild look in them that I haven't seen before. Scrambling to my feet, I swallow against the lump in my throat. It's really happening.

"Quickly love, get dressed," Will orders.

Rushing to the desk to retrieve my clothes from where I left them last night, I quickly pull on the black pants, lace them, and slip on the loose white shirt. I button it and tuck it tightly into the pants. That is one of Will's top tips, never allow your enemy the chance to grab hold of you. Shoving my feet into my boots, I quickly tie my hair back and turn to face Will. He is waiting, weapons belt in hand. Deftly, he fastens it around my hips. It is stocked with my short, slim sword and an assortment of daggers ranging from a couple small ones for throwing, to a large, wicked-looking dagger with a curved blade. I sway slightly, not accustomed to the weight of so many weapons.

My heart is hammering inside my ribs. I can feel the heat in my cheeks, the sweat beading on my upper lip. The adrenaline and terror coursing through my veins are one hell of a combination. I look up at him with wide eyes, searching his face for...what am I looking for, exactly? Reassurance? Strength? But he can't give me either of those things now. I must find my own strength. Today I must be my own hero.

"Will?" My voice doesn't sound right to my own ears.

I'm not entirely sure what I was going to say next, but it doesn't matter anyway, because his arms are around me, pulling me roughly to his chest. And then his lips are on mine. It's the kind of kiss that could fix even the most broken of hearts. But right now, it is what is breaking mine. Will pulls away, leaving me breathless.

"Are you ready?" he whispers.

"No," I reply as a tear slips down my cheek.

"Neither am I," he presses one last quick kiss against my lips, and then he runs to the door, throws it open, and is gone.

For a long moment I just stand there, scared, stunned. A deep breath in and out steadies my nerves some, and then I am running too.

By the time I am out the door, the crew has already assembled on the deck. There is an uneasy silence hanging over the Jolly Roger. Making my way through the crowd of men, I find Will at the front of the group, his gaze fixed on the horizon. Miles stands at his side; the two men are a force to be reckoned with all on their own. Backed by the crew, it is hard to imagine them losing a fight. Surprisingly, I find Cash standing on Will's other side. If we all make it through this fight, maybe the three of us can actually be friends. When I approach the three men, Cash turns to me and with a small nod makes room for me beside Will. Slipping my hand into Will's, I fix my gaze on the horizon and wait.

Time passes but nothing happens. The only sounds are the sails snapping in the wind and the waves crashing against the hull of the ship. I'm beginning to get restless. Shifting my weight from one foot to the other, I wonder if the warning bells were a bit premature. But then, a familiar sound drifts across the water. Mermaids. Their song fills the air casting an eerie feeling over the scene. Every hair on my arms stands up as chills ripple through my body. Then the shouting starts.

Tearing his hand from mine, Will reaches for his sword. I can't see anything; I have no clue what is happening out there. The mermaid's song morphs into the awful screeching they make out of water. Hearing the two sounds simultaneously is unnerving to say the least, and mixed with the shouts, it has put a terrifying picture into my head of what could be happening out there. Shading my eyes with my hand, I look out across the water, hoping to catch a glimpse of what is going on, but no matter how hard I squint or strain my eyes, I see nothing.

A gun goes off behind me, followed closely by two cannons. Aiden and the fairies have arrived. Looking up, I see them swarming towards the ship. And there, circling above the massive army of fairies, is Aiden. Beside me, Will draws his sword. The sounds of the mermaids drown out the sound of wings even as the swarm of fairies draws nearer. Turning to Will I grab his arm, forcing him to look at me.

"I love you," I shout over the sound of gunfire. The words are rushed, but I had to say them, just in case.

He looks down at me. "I know," he says with a small smile. "I love you, too."

Flashes of light signal the arrival of fairies on the ship. Tearing my eyes from Will's, I see them shifting all over the deck. Half their host is still in the air, but we are already outnumbered. Scanning the ship, I don't see Aiden anywhere, but I know he's here, I can feel it. I turn back to where Will had been standing beside me, but he has already thrown himself into the mix of pirates and fairies on the deck. Sliding one of the smaller daggers from my belt with one hand, and my slender sword with the other, I too plunge into what will be my first and last battle.

There are fairies everywhere, some in their larger forms fighting with magic against the steel of the pirates. Most though are still in their tiny forms, hurling magic into the clusters of people with no regard for who they hit. The sounds of mermaids and the shouting on the water have either stopped, or just can't be heard anymore. Gunshots go off across the ship. The smell of the gunpowder assaults my nostrils just as the sound of a body hitting the water reaches my ears. More gunshots—a dead fairy drops to the deck at my feet and my stomach heaves.

I look at the carnage around me, the bodies of fairies raining from the sky, the pirates fighting, already covered in blood. My senses have gone into overdrive. I am frozen in place.

Move! A little voice in my head hisses. *Move, Elena!* I

cannot just stand uselessly by anymore. Then I see him, Aiden, across the deck slicing at pirates with that wicked dagger of his. I have to get to him; I have to end this once and for all. Moving quickly across the deck, I begin to make my way to the green-eyed boy.

A fairy dives from above, the flash of light as he shifts blinding me temporarily. Then he is on me, tackling me to the ground. The sweet, spicy scent of magic fills my nose, chokes me, just as his hands wrap around the exposed skin of my throat. A bloodcurdling scream bursts from my lips. My skin is burning. The magic wreathing the fairy's hands sizzles against my flesh and I cannot stop screaming. I dropped both of my weapons when he tackled me leaving me utterly defenseless. Thrashing on the deck, I claw at his arms, his hands, his face. Anything to make it stop. The smell of burning flesh and magic is cloying, sickening. This can't be how it ends.

But then the fairy is gone. No longer pinned down, I roll to my knees, gasping and gingerly touching the ruined skin that he left behind. Hands are under my arms now, hauling me to my feet. Cash's face enters my vision, it is splattered with blood and streaked black with soot and gunpowder. His golden curls hang in his eyes, eyes that are now taking in my charred skin.

"Elena, get out of here! Run!" he yells over the chaos pointing towards the captain's quarters.

I blink dumbly at him, trying to clear my head. No, I can't run. I will not run. Carefully, I crouch to retrieve my weapons from where I dropped them. When I stand again, I shake my head at him. I won't run.

"This is a terrible idea," Cash shakes his head, turning away from me, his own sword in hand.

I try to tell him that I am staying, but it's too painful to talk. I don't have to talk to fight though. Another gunshot goes off, much too close for comfort, followed by another tiny body hitting the deck with a sickening crunch. Closing my eyes, I suck in one deep, steadying breath through my nose. When my eyes open again, I am focused, ready. Glancing around, I see a pirate being overwhelmed by fairies. They buzz around him, biting, clawing, burning through his flesh with their magic. Setting off in the direction of the pirate, I adjust my grip on my weapons, but before I can get to him, he is gone, his lifeless body dropping to the deck. The fairies disperse immediately, off to find their next target. Rage and determination burn inside me. I know these men, I have lived with them, eaten with them, trained with them and now they are dying around me.

I desperately want to find Will, but there is so much chaos, it would be nearly impossible.

Focus, Elena, the voice in my head tells me.

Right. Getting to Aiden is the most important goal. The odds are that if I find Aiden, I will also find Will. My eyes scan the ship again, searching through the smoke from the cannons.

There, that voice stops my search.

Right in the center of the ship, in the worst of the carnage, I see Will's dark head and Aiden's lighter one. The sun reflects off their weapons as they stab and slice with sword and dagger. *Go*, the voice urges.

Each step across the deck makes my head and my

throat throb unbearably. But still I run. Spotting a fairy in her larger form off to my left about to deal a fatal blow to one of the crew, I stop long enough to hurl the small dagger in my hand, hoping it at least hits the fairy. I never got much practice with the throwing knives. My technique is off, so it is the handle of the dagger that hits her in the shoulder instead of the blade. The knife drops to the deck with a clang. It's enough though. The pirate turns at the sound, dispatches the fairy with one swipe of his sword, and sprints away.

I am running again, gaining ground, getting closer to my target. Will and Aiden are still at the center of everything, circling each other. Both men are panting, both are bleeding from wounds I can see more clearly as I draw nearer. The acrid smell of charred flesh hangs heavy in the air, stinging my nose with every painful gasp for air. Cannons go off, three of them this time. Boats filled with children, their faces so young and scared, flash through my mind. No, I cannot worry about that now. There are much bigger things I need to focus on now.

I am within twenty feet of Aiden and Will when a familiar fairy steps into my path. Her face is smug, green eyes full of amusement. Tatiana places her hands on her hips.

"Well, well...look who I found," she singsongs in that irritating, high pitched voice of hers.

Oh, I hate her. I don't bother trying to respond. My palms are slick; I have to maneuver my weapons around to wipe them on my pants. The hilts of the weapons are cool against my skin. Adjusting my grip, I narrow my eyes at the fairy. She giggles. She actually *giggles*. My vision goes red and black.

"You really think you have any chance against me, Elena?" Tatiana taunts. "I have magic, I can shift forms, *and* I can fly! I am better than you in every way!"

I launch myself at her, sword and dagger raised and ready. Tatiana spins out of my path and all my dagger hits is air.

"You see, stupid girl, you cannot win!" she continues with a triumphant smile.

But this fight has only just begun, and I am going to enjoy this immensely. I ready myself and charge at her again. This time she shifts in a blinding flash of light, reappearing behind me, her delicate wings keeping her aloft. Why won't she just fight me? Then it hits me. Maybe she is scared to actually fight me. She is all bark and no bite. Or maybe...maybe she is just reluctant to kill me because of what Aiden would do to her. He wants me after all, needs me. If she killed me, he would have to find someone new for his ritual, and I can't imagine he would be very happy about that.

I can play this to my advantage, use her temper against her. If I can get her worked up enough, maybe, just maybe...

"If you're so confident that you can beat me, why do you keep running?" I spit the question like venom, despite the agony each word causes as it escapes my ruined throat.

Tatiana stiffens, her little pointed face going red. Unfortunately, she regains her composure more quickly than I had hoped.

"Who says that I am running?" Tatiana sneers. "Perhaps I just like seeing you make a fool out of yourself."

"At least I'm *trying* to fight," I fire back. "All you do is shift and avoid me. I am starting to think you can't beat me at all. I think that maybe you're just a coward." That does the trick.

Tatiana's rage takes over her then. She lets out a horrible sound, somewhere between a growl and a scream, shifting mid-shriek. Blinking against the flash of light, I stumble back a few steps. The fairy tackles me to the deck, her face twisted with anger. She looks positively feral. Even in her human form, she is smaller than I am, but still, she manages to pin me. She beats at me with small fists, getting in a couple of decent blows to my face and my already ruined neck. Her knees dig painfully into my sides.

My right arm covers my face, taking the brunt of the hits Tatiana deals out, but I don't fight back. Instead I let her wear herself out, let her waste her energy. She could easily use her magic on me, burn my skin with it, even kill me with it. But she doesn't. Is she so lost in her rage that she hasn't thought about it? Or can she truly not kill me? I lost my sword when she tackled me, but the fingers of my left hand are still clutched around the hilt of my dagger.

"I hate you!" she hisses, over and over, as she continues to beat at me.

Well, Tatiana, the feeling is mutual, I think, and then I strike, slamming my knees into the fairy's back. She loses her balance and I buck my hips, throwing her to the side. I roll to my hands and knees, the dagger still in my fist. Tatiana tries to drag herself away, but I grab her by one leg and yank her back.

"No!" she screams, her fingers scrabbling for something to hold onto.

Shuffling on my knees until I tower over the fairy, I flip her over and pin her just as she had me, straddling her, knees digging into her sides. There, mixed with the rage on her face, that's the fear I've been eager to see. And it is quickly becoming the more dominant emotion in her body. But as the look of fear grows, Tatiana's hands begin to glow, the magic wreathing her fingers like green flame and smoke. This is going to hurt...

I manage to pin one of her arms to the deck with my knee. She thrashes beneath me, trying to buck me off, but unless I let go of my weapon, I can't pin the other. She grabs onto my forearm and the pain is instantaneous. My skin sizzles everywhere that the swirling magic licks at it, but I can't let her up. Gritting my teeth against my screams, I raise my left hand and plunge the curved dagger into the fairy's chest. Her green eyes go wide, her mouth forming a little "O" as I pull the dagger out, and plunge it in again, a guttural scream ripping itself from my injured throat.

The magic wrapped around her hands dissipates, and her fingers loosen, her arm dropping to her side with a thud. Tatiana gasps, her chest heaving up and down beneath me, but I remain straddled over her body. I'm too paranoid to move. This could be another of her tricks and if I move, she might bounce back up, magically healed as soon as she is free. Besides, this is personal, I want to watch the life leave her eyes. Tatiana's lips are moving, but I can't hear what she is saying. Over and over, she repeats the same thing. I lean down, careful to keep her immobile, and put my ear to her mouth, curious what she could possibly be saying. It is not what I expected.

"Aiden." Over and over the fairy whispers his name.

It's not what she is saying that surprises me, more how she says it. Because even while she bleeds out on the deck of the ship, slowly dying, I can hear the loyalty and love for him in her whispers. Rising up, I watch her lips slow, the silence between her wet breaths gets longer. Until finally, she goes still. Tatiana's eyes are unblinking, staring up at the sky while her blood pools around her, leaving her in a crimson puddle on the deck.

Slowly, I rise to my feet, barely aware of the battle still raging around me. Everything seems muffled, almost as if I'm underwater. I can hear the sounds of weapons clashing, of men cursing, of gunshots and cannon fire, but it all seems very far away. Glancing down at my arm I see that burned into the sleeve of my shirt, and into the soft flesh beneath, is a perfect handprint. If I survive, the scar it will probably leave will serve as a constant reminder of the life I just so violently took. And what's even worse? I don't regret it, not even a little bit. Letting my injured arm drop to my side, I stoop to grab my sword and turn away from Tatiana's body, not even bothering to take the dagger from where it protrudes from her chest.

The boy can feel it when she dies. Stupid fairy had to go and get herself killed. Now there will be no one on his side, no one at his back. No matter, she can be replaced easily enough. The boy always has a backup plan.

A few feet away, his brother, the legendary pirate captain of the Jolly Roger paces. Sweat drips from the pirate's brow, leaving streaks down his dirty, smoke stained face.

"Is that all you've got, brother?" Will spits.

The boy can feel his magic sputtering, erratic and out of control, but still, his lips tug up into a smile.

"No," he says. "Not even close."

CHAPTER 9

I am cutting my way across the deck of the Jolly Roger, fighting to the center of the chaos. Fighting my way to Will. I stopped feeling anything a long time ago, or maybe it was only a moment ago; time stopped existing for me the moment I turned away from Tatiana's corpse. Tatiana was not my first kill, I killed Aiden before, even if he didn't stay dead. Now I am killing again. Fairies, both small and human sized drop around me, dead by my blades, or by others'. I don't feel remorse for them anymore. I see nothing but my target, the prize at the end of this sick, twisted, deadly game. Killing Aiden. Hate and rage are the only thing keeping me going now. Bloodlust has taken over all of my senses.

Another fairy steps into my path, hands glowing red with magic. Aside from her reddish-gold hair, she looks a bit like Tatiana. It doesn't matter; she will fall too. The fairy girl cups her hands together, a ball of red fire forming between her palms. I don't stop. She releases the fireball in her palms, throwing it straight in my direction. Jumping to the side, the magic sizzles past me, singeing the front of my white shirt. The smell of burned cotton reaches my nose, mixing with the smell of cannon smoke and gunpowder. Wrinkling my nose at the unpleasant assault, I begin stalking across the wooden planks again. A fresh ball of magic is already forming between the fairy's hands. Her face is set with determination, teeth gritted and bared. But she is not quick enough. Before she can unleash her magic upon me again, I am on her. My blade goes through the flesh of her abdomen like a hot knife through butter. Using all my strength, I push the sword through until the point is protruding grotesquely from her back.

The fairy girl has pink eyes. I only notice their color when they go dull, her life fading away as I pull the sword out. Her body hits the deck with a heavy thud. Stepping over her lifeless form, I continue on my path to the center of the chaos.

The pirate watches his brother smirk a few feet away, twirling that wicked dagger in his hand. The jeweled handle still shines even under the coating of blood and grime. The deck of his beautiful ship is slick with too much blood, Will can smell its metallic tang all around him. Smoke and sweat sting his eyes. No matter, the amount of fairy bodies strewn about makes it seem as though his side is winning this battle. If only he could get close enough to bury his hook in the soft spot between his brother's shoulder and his neck.

But his brother is quick and crafty. He manages to

dodge every blow, block every strike. If he can just wear Aiden down, exhaust his energy and magic, then he can end this once and for all. Will hopes that Elena is alright. She too is fighting somewhere on this ship, and Will prays that she is still breathing. He cannot lose focus to look for her though. If he tears his eyes away from this battle, his own personal battle, it could be the end of him.

So the pirate continues to circle the king of Neverland. It is a sort of sick, twisted dance the two of them are performing, surrounded by death and chaos.

Cash is soaked through with sweat and blood; some of it is his own, most of it isn't. Not far from him, a pirate falls, swarmed by little fairies. There is nothing he could have done to help the man. Cash is in the middle of fighting his own battle. Surrounded by fairies, both large and small, he turns slowly in a circle, careful not to keep his back to any for too long. He is vastly outnumbered and has almost no training or experience when it comes to fights. Things are not looking good for him at the moment. Cash assumes that it is pure luck that has kept him alive this long, but he will continue to fight. He says a silent prayer, hoping that his luck doesn't run out too soon.

I can see my targets, one dark head and one light; they are only a few feet away now. The two men are circling each other. Suddenly, one strikes out, just for the other to deflect. This is it. I must make it to Aiden and kill him. Just a little further. Just a few more steps. The men are so close and yet so far away. All I can see is Aiden's face. My vision is so tunneled that I don't notice at first. I don't notice the green glow surrounding Aiden's hands, his magic burning and pulsing. I don't see it until Aiden lifts one of those glowing hands and tosses a ball of glowing green fire directly into Will's chest.

My feet stop moving. My heart stops beating. My world stops.

There is the most devastating look of pain on Will's face when he turns his head in my direction. How does he know where I'm standing? Someone is screaming in the distance. Or maybe the one screaming is me, I don't know. And then Will crumples to the ground, falls onto his side, and does not move again.

There is a slight throb in my knees. Did I fall? The stench of charred flesh fills my nose. Whose skin is burning? My stomach roils, then deposits itself onto the deck. I vomit until my stomach is empty, and then I climb to my feet and lock eyes with Aiden. The smile on his face would be terrifying if I still felt fear, but all I feel right now is rage. Sprinting past Will's body, I launch myself at Aiden. He catches me in the air and tosses me aside like nothing. Standing over me, Aiden presses the ball of one bare foot into the ruined skin of my neck. Black spots dance across my vision as I writhe in pain beneath him. I sink my nails into Aiden's foot causing him to jerk away, kicking me in the face when he does.

Taking advantage of the momentary opening, I scramble backwards until my back hits something hard.

Will's body lies just a few feet in front of me, his eyes are closed and he is completely still. I am vaguely aware that around me the chaos has stopped. Someone is saying my name, over and over. Hands are on either side of my face, a pair of eyes are looking into mine. The eyes are wild, full of fear and shock.

"Elena," the voice is saying. "Elena!"

It sounds so far away, or like they are underwater. Or maybe I am underwater. Maybe I am drowning and all of this is just a hallucination due to the lack of oxygen getting to my brain. I cannot tear my eyes from the body on the deck. Will's body. Will...

There are hands underneath my arms, someone is trying to haul me up. My legs are not working. The hands are hauling me across the deck now. Dragging me away from Will's unmoving body. I don't want to leave Will. Why are they taking me away?The hands suddenly disappear. Falling back, the back of my head slams into the wood of the deck. It does not hurt; I feel no pain. I don't even feel the rage anymore. All that's left is grief and a gnawing emptiness.

Arms are scooping me up, lifting me. I am floating; it feels like flying. Maybe I am flying.

Will is not dead. He can't be dead. Stunned, he was just stunned. Will cannot be dead. Why does it look like the clouds are getting closer? Will can't be dead. Turning my head to the side, I do not see him like I expected to. Instead I see the crow's nest. I look the other direction, and Aiden's blurry face, his golden, wavy hair, bright green eyes, all begin to come to the surface. He has me cradled like a baby in his arms.

I *am* flying. Where is Will? I've changed my mind. I don't think Will is alive. If he were alive, he would have fought for me. He would not have let Aiden take me. But Aiden did take me, so Will must be dead. Cradled in Aiden's arms, I am drifting further away from the Jolly Roger, away from the death and carnage left behind from the battle, and away from Will. No, Will is not dead, he's not! He will come for me!

Looking out across the Never Sea, there is something in the distance, something familiar. Oh...

Skull Rock looms in the distance, the gaping mouth and eyes seem to be mocking me, like a morbid reminder of what is going to happen to me. All the memories come rushing back. I remember the stone altar in the heart of the cave. I remember Aiden tossing me onto it, preparing for the ritual, that long, jeweled dagger glowing in the dim candlelight.

It's all going to happen again, and this time Will might not make it in time to save me. I failed in my last attempt at attacking Aiden. He might not be able to use his magic against me, but even without it, I don't think I can beat him without a miracle. If I can just hold on until Will arrives then everything will be fine.

Cash hears the screaming and knows immediately what happened. The pirate captain has fallen. Elena's screams are deafening, heart breaking. She really does love him. Cash cannot fault her for that. She hurt him, yes, but she really loves the pirate. Cash turns, sees

Elena fall to her knees, sees her vomiting onto the deck. He starts to go to her, but she pushes herself to her feet and takes off, launching herself at Aiden. Before she so much as touches him, Aiden tosses her aside. She hits the deck hard before the boy proceeds to place his foot on her throat. Cash can't help but wince when he sees her writing beneath the boy. He can't stand by and watch Aiden kill Elena, but the odds of him winning a fight against Aiden are very slim.

Elena grabs Aiden's foot and he jerks away, giving her the chance to scramble back until her back hits the mast. Then Cash is running to her. By the time he reaches her, Aiden is already sauntering their direction. He kneels before Elena, not caring about the blood soaking through the knees of his pants.

"Elena!" Cash says her name again and again. "Get up!"

She doesn't respond. Her eyes stare blankly, there's no life behind them anymore, there's no emotion on her face. Cash looks over his shoulder to where Will's body lays. The man has not moved, but there does not appear to be much blood around him. Magic then. Perhaps he is not truly dead.

Aiden has almost reached them now; his glowing eyes are intent on Elena. The simple crown that he wears is slightly askew atop his head. Quickly, Cash jumps to his feet and attempts to haul her to her feet. He must get her away from the boy. She will not move! Cash begins to drag her backwards across the deck. She doesn't fight him, but she does not exactly make it any easier for him either.

Aiden is able to move much faster than Cash, he prowls towards them with a sinister grin on his blood-spattered face. Sweat pours down Cash's face, but he forces himself to move faster still. Looking up, Cash is surprised to see that Aiden is no longer coming after them. Aiden is nowhere to be seen at all.

"Boo."

The whisper in Cash's ear startles him so much that he drops Elena. She falls back, her head slamming on the deck with a sickening thud. Cash whirls around to find Aiden standing there with a familiar jeweled dagger in his hand. Cash dropped his own weapon when he ran for Elena, not that it matters. Even if he still had it, he wouldn't have the chance to use it before Aiden uses the butt of his pretty blade to bash him in the temple, and then everything goes black.

The boy is losing the fight against his brother. Yes, the boy has magic, but it is far too unreliable at the moment. The magic that normally zings through his veins is only a mere fizzle now, guttering like a candle in the wind. Without his magic, well, the boy honestly does not think he possesses the hand to hand combat skills that his brother does; he could be bested, and that simply cannot happen. The pirate strikes at him once, twice. The boy dodges and parries the attacks. If he does not act now, he will lose this fight, and this time, it will be his true end. The fairy is dead; she will not be there to save him again. The boy is not sure if any of the other fairies are powerful enough to perform that sort of magic, or if they would be willing. The other fairies are loyal to him, but only because they fear his power. Without it, he doesn't know how long that loyalty would last.

The boy had always counted on the love that Tatiana had for him. That's why he made her his right hand in the first place. Of course, she was one of the strongest fairies in Neverland, but her unyielding love for him is what really made her stand out. He had always used Tatiana's love to his advantage and to get what he wanted. But Tatiana got herself killed, so now he can only rely on himself and the small bit of magic sputtering in his veins. That magic is now curling itself around his fingers, building, concentrating in his palms. It will take almost all of it to kill his brother, but it will be worth it.

Aiden curls the fingers of his left hand, the magic forming into a pulsing ball. The pirate is so focused on killing him that he has not even noticed the green glow of the magic. He also does not notice when the boy turns his wrist, raises his hand, and fires that ball of magic directly at the pirate's chest.

The bloodcurdling screams that begin as soon as he releases his magic are priceless, almost as priceless as the look of shock and fear on his brother's face when the magic punches into his chest. Aiden turns just in time to see Elena fall, just in time to hear the crack of her knees as they hit the deck. A grin stretches across the boy's face as Elena doubles over and vomits onto the deck of Will's beloved ship. There is something so poetic about killing a man on his own ship.

Elena rises to her feet and rushes at him, but Aiden simply tosses her aside before pressing his foot into her ruined throat. He takes great pleasure in watching her writhe in pain beneath him. But when she digs her finger-nails into his foot, all amusement fades. Jerking away, Aiden stumbles back giving, Elena time to scramble away. The blond boy rushes to help her, tries to drag her away, but he cannot save her now, no one can.

William faces off with his brother one last time. The fight has been going on for far too long; he should have ended it by now. Will knows he can beat his brother. Aiden may have magic, but it is waning, and with Will's superior fighting skills, he is sure to win. But the pirate also knows that the boy is clever, tricky. He knows that he must be ready for anything. Despite all of Will's fighting skill and graceful movements, despite all of his knowledge about the boy and his ways, the pirate does not see it coming.

Will doesn't know what is happening until the ball of magic is hurtling toward him. There is no time to react, to even try to dodge the blow. The magic punches into his chest and the pain is instantaneous. Will looks down, touches the tips of his fingers to the gaping wound. He hears her scream and turns his head to look at her. The look of horror and despair on her face would break Will's heart, if his heart had not been scorched by a magic fireball. God, she is so beautiful, even when she is falling apart. At least he gets to see the girl he loves one last time before he dies.

I feel a small jolt and know that we have reached Skull Rock. Peering around Aiden's shoulder, I search the horizon for any sign of Will or the Jolly Roger but there is nothing. *Please hurry Will*, I think. I don't know how long I can last against Aiden. I am so tired and cold; every inch of me hurts. Aiden speaks but I'm not listening. I am so cold that I'm shivering, but he feels so warm. I can't resist laying my cheek against his chest.

Aiden speaks again. Looking up at him, I see what looks like affection in his eyes. No, I must be mistaken, Aiden doesn't feel anything for me, or for anyone except himself. Swaying gently as Aiden walks, as he carries me to my death, I close my eyes and think of Will. He will save me; I just have to hold on a little longer.

Elena is so beautiful; it truly is a shame that he has to kill her. She would look so lovely by his side. But his magic is much more important to him than any girl, even a girl as wonderfully fierce as Elena. He saw her during the battle on the ship, he watched as she cut down fairy after fairy, he saw the bloodlust in her eyes. This beautiful girl with bright hair that matches the fire in her soul is much more like him than she would ever admit.

"Elena," the boy says. "Are you awake?"

Her skin is so cold, he can feel it through her tattered shirt. Goosebumps erupt across his body. Hazel eyes meet his and something in his heart twists. There is no sign of fire in Elena's eyes anymore, no life in them at all. There is only despair, defeat, and acceptance of what is going to happen to her.

"You are so beautiful." He cannot resist saying it.

Elena is not listening anyway. Closing her eyes, Elena rests her cheek against his chest and does not look up at him again.

The swaying stops after a while; Aiden has stopped walking. The warmth of his body is replaced with cool air, and then cool stone against my back as he lays me down on the altar at the center of the cave. Staring up at the stone above me, I can hear Aiden moving around the cave. He is chanting softly. I let my head drop to the side to find him lighting candles as he makes his way around. He has started the ritual that will end my life and prolong his even further.

There is still no sign of Will. Maybe he's not coming after all. Maybe he really is dead, just like I will be soon. If that is my fate, I wish it would just be over already, because if Will is dead, then I would prefer to go into death with him rather than live in a world without him in it. I close my eyes, hoping that I will be reunited with him soon.

Cash comes back to consciousness to find that a new sort of chaos has erupted aboard the Jolly Roger. Elena is gone, Aiden took her, flew off with her, after Cash's failed attempt to save her. The fairies started to disperse as well, flying off after their king. In their wake, only carnage and destruction remain.

Cash does not know what to do next, so he feels incredibly relieved when the exceptionally large first mate, Mr. Miles, takes control. Rushing to his fallen captain, the man barks at the crew, ordering some to clear the deck of bodies and blood, some to tend to their wounded friends, and some to get the ship moving. They are going to go after Elena and Aiden. Miles takes it upon himself to scoop up the body of his fallen captain and rush him inside. Cash was not given any instructions, and not knowing what else to do, he follows Miles into the dark interior of the ship. He walks through the door just as the large man is laying Will down on the bed.

"Boy!" the first mate calls to him. "Get over here and help me!"

Cash hesitates briefly before his legs begin to move and in seconds he is standing over the captain's body looking down at a gaping hole in the man's chest. There is no possible way to save him, no way that he could possibly survive a wound like that. But he will do as Miles asks. For Elena, and for his own conscience, he will do what he can to save Will.

"Towels and water, now!" Miles orders.

Cash wants to argue with the man, he wants to tell him that he does not think that will work, but he does as the man asks anyway. Cash rushes into the bathing chamber, grabbing a stack of towels from the shelf on the wall. A bucket of water sits on the floor, most likely left over from someone's last bath. He gathers his supplies and a few seconds later, Cash is standing beside the bed, soaking towels in the water and handing them over per Miles's orders. This close, the smell of charred flesh is enough to make Cash gag, but he does not allow the pirate to see. Instead, he watches quietly while Miles meticulously cleans the raw, jagged edges of Will's wound. "Get a shirt," Miles growls. "Tear it into pieces, I need to pack the wound." Cash does as he says, though he cannot resist speaking up.

"Is he even breathing?" Cash asks, handing strips of cloth to the first mate.

Miles's hands pause their work.

"I do not know," he replies quietly. "I shall find out once I get this wound packed."

"Fair enough," Cash shrugs, ripping another strip from the shirt.

When the last piece of cloth has been stuffed into the hole in the captain's chest, Miles stops and stares down at his friend's unmoving form. He does not move, only stares. Clearly, he does not know what to do next. But unfortunately for Cash, he does know what to do.

"Move," Cash says.

The pirate turns, looking up at him with a rather confused look on his face. Cash rolls his eyes.

"Move," he repeats, more forcefully this time.

The first mate scrambles off the bed to his feet. He moves aside to make room for Cash, who kneels on the bed besides Will's body. He leans down, lays his head on the man's chest, listens for a heartbeat, but feels nothing. He places his hand in front of Will's mouth, two fingers beneath his nose, checking for breath.

There, he can feel it. The pirate's breathing is weak and

very irregular, but it is there. Lucky for Miles, and for Will, Cash knows CPR. It will be difficult to perform with the hole in his chest and all, but Cash will try. Elena will be devastated if Will dies, that is, if she survives. Placing one hand on Will's chest, the other hand on top of it, Cash hopes that they will not be too late. Then he begins the grueling process of trying to save a life.

Inside the cave at Skull rock, the boy has begun the ritual that will return all of his powers to him, restore his strength, and stop the aging that has been plaguing him for months now. Aiden feels practically ancient now. On the stone altar, Elena lays silently, staring up at the roof of the cave. She has not made a sound since she stopped screaming aboard the Jolly Roger. It is rather unsettling.

The boy circles the cave, lighting candles as he goes and repeating the words of the spell that will save his life. He will draw upon the candles for power, and when Elena's blood has been drained, he will take her remaining years for himself. In a small alcove of the cave, the boy gathers the bone bowls that will collect her blood and carries them to the altar in the center. He places one on each side of the altar, looking down at his victim as he circles around. It is not nearly as much fun when she is not frightened, when she is not fighting back.

The boy flips her hands over to expose the soft, delicate skin of her forearms. He makes sure that her fingertips hang off the edge of the altar, just above the bone bowls. Still, she does not move or speak. Drawing his dagger, Aiden takes one of Elena's hands in his. The colorful jewels in the daggers handle reflect the light of the candles, sending a rainbow projecting onto the grey stone walls. Elena does not so much as flinch when the blade touches her skin. She does not even blink or gasp when the blade pierces through the tender flesh of her arm. Frowning slightly, the boy drags the blade straight down her forearm, ruby blood welling in its wake. He checks that the blood is being collected properly in the bowl below, repositions it, and moves to the other side.

Repeating the process, the boy steps back to admire his work. Blood flows in red rivulets from the long, deep gashes in Elena's arms. Soon, very soon, he will be feeling much better.

Cash has been working on the pirate captain for what feels like an eternity. Sweat is beading on his upper lip and forehead, stinging his eyes as it drips down his face. But he cannot stop. Will is still breathing, although it feels as though his temperature is dropping a bit, but Cash will not stop until the pirate is cold *and* no longer breathing at all.

Behind him, Cash knows Miles is watching vigilantly, waiting for a verdict on whether his friend will live or die. Cash's arms ache and burn, his muscles straining against the effort of keeping Will's heart pumping. But he does not stop, he will not stop until there is no hope left.

All I can see is the stone roof of the cave. I stare up at it, vaguely aware of Aiden still moving around me, he is still chanting the same thing over and over. Then his face appears in my line of sight, those green eyes burning down at me. Cool steel touches my arm, bites into my skin. I can feel the blade slice down one arm, then the other shortly after. It does not even hurt. What is wrong with me? My arms feel warm, wet, but there is no pain, so I do not move. My legs are getting cold. So is my face, my torso, but my arms are still so warm.

Fight, I should be fighting back, but there is no fire left inside of me. All of that rage, all of that bloodlust and anger and desire to fight and kill...it's all gone. Everything inside of me shut down the second I saw Will fall. Will. He never came for me; he didn't rescue me. That must mean that he's dead. So, I continue to lay on the stone slab inside of the cave, and stare up, wishing I could see the stars one last time before I die too.

CHAPTER 10

I am floating. Everything is fuzzy—my sight, my hearing—my limbs are tingling. I am no longer cold. Instead I feel warm, blissfully warm actually. It feels as though I am floating in a warm bath. Nothing hurts, not even my heart. The smell of the sea in the distance is comforting. The scent of salt and wind makes me feel like Will is here with me, like I am wrapped in his arms again. I am not scared.

Will, I say silently, *I will see you soon*.

The bowls are almost full, which means that Elena is almost dead. Soon the boy will have everything he wants again. The pirate captain is dead, Aiden will have full use of his powers again, and everything will be as it should be.

Circling the altar in the center of Skull Rock, the boy

looks down at Elena. Even in the warm candlelight, her skin is eerily pale. Her hair seems impossibly bright splayed around her head, like a halo of fire. There is a blue tinge to her lips, lips he once kissed in another cave behind the waterfall in his favorite place. That night seems so long ago, and yet, he remembers it so clearly. Aiden did not have to take her there, to his favorite part of the island. Never before had he taken any girl there, not since *her*. Not since Wendy.

Memories flash through the boy's mind, sharp and painful as knives. She had the most beautiful blonde curls he has ever seen. Something inside of him twists, bringing him crashing to his knees in the sand. Her eyes were so deep blue that even the ocean would be envious. Her skin was flawless, like porcelain.

It was not just her looks that had made the boy fall so hard for her though. Her soul had been as beautiful as her appearance, possibly even more so. Wendy had been kind, caring, generous. She had the most delicious sense of adventure that the boy could not help but love. Like Elena, Wendy had possessed a certain fire that was simply irresistible. Maybe that is why he is so fond of the girl bleeding out before him.

Shakily, the boy tries to rise to his feet, only to be brought back down by another memory, this one much darker.

Wendy stood across from him on the deck of the Jolly Roger, terror filling her eyes. The pirate's hook was at her throat, his other hand on her waist. Rage filled him up to the point of bursting. The boy should have cut off that hand too when he had the chance.

"Not another step," the pirate growled. "Or I will cut her throat."

"You wouldn't dare," the boy hissed, narrowing his eyes.

"Go on then, if you're so confident, come and get her." The pirate pressed the point of his hook into Wendy's throat, just over her artery.

Every muscle in his body was telling him to move, to get her back. But he did not dare, for even though he did not truly believe that the pirate would kill Wendy, there was no telling just how deep the darkness ran inside of his brother.

"Alright," the boy held up his hands, took a step back. "You win. Let her go."

The pirate hesitated, dropped the hook just low enough to give the boy the time to grab the bow and a single arrow from its place on his back. Nocking the arrow, the boy aimed and fired before the pirate had a chance to react, but in his rage, either his aim was off, or the pirate had moved just in time.

The arrow struck home, in Wendy's heart. Blood bloomed around the shaft, soaking through the blue dress that complimented her eyes so well.

"No!" the boy roared the word. But it was too late. Her eyes went wide, and then she fell lifeless to the deck of the Jolly Roger.

The pirate raised his arms. "Brother..." he started.

"Do not say a word, pirate," the boy spit the words like venom. "I hate you! More so now than ever before!" A tear, just one, slid from his eye. "I no longer have a brother. You will pay!" The boy ripped the quiver of arrows from his back and tossed it into the sea. He then snapped the bow over his knee and flung it away too before rocketing into the night sky. From that day on, he had sworn never to touch a bow and arrow again.

The boy's eyes open. He is on his hands and knees in the sand. Lifting his head, the boy crawls to the altar a few feet away. He catches sight of his reflection in the blood, now practically overflowing the edge of the bone bowl. Haggard, that is the best way to describe himself at the moment. And *old*! The aging is happening much more quickly. Only a thin trickle of crimson liquid drips from Elena's pale arm.

Reaching up, the boy uses the edge of the stone slab to pull himself to his feet. Elena is perfectly still, her eyes staring blankly up at nothing. Pale, she is so pale. The boy reaches out a shaking hand to touch her face. Her skin is like ice. When he places his hand over her heart, he finds that it is no longer beating. Dead, Elena is dead, just like his brother, just like Wendy, just like Tatiana. He is alone in the world for the first time, and the feeling is quite unsettling.

No, he cannot possibly be that weak. It's his magic, he has never let it deplete so much, that must be what is causing these ridiculous thoughts.

Aiden lifts one bowl, carrying it to the alcove across the cave. In his rush, blood sloshes over the edge. No matter, he has what he needs. He hastily sets the first bowl down then retrieves the other. A trail of dark droplets stains the sand spanning the distance between the alcove and altar. Aiden spares one last glance at the dead girl. As he turns away, that same something twists inside of him.

Rushing to the alcove, Aiden almost trips, but catches himself before the precious blood can spill onto the sand. He quickly sets it next to the other and draws his dagger. Dragging it across his palm, he lets his own blood mix with hers, infusing it with magic. A faint glow emanates from each bowl, a sign that it is ready. Lifting one bowl very carefully to his lips, the boy gulps down a few mouthfuls of the magically infused blood before pouring what remains over his head while repeating the spell. Repeating the process with the second bowl until he is covered head to toe with crimson blood. The boy smiles as power soaks into his skin. His body is growing stronger, the aging has halted, he can feel it. The magic he so loves zings through his veins once more. He stretches his limbs, feeling much better, more like himself. The first time he performed this ritual, it was disgusting and he vomited blood for hours afterwards. Now though, he almost enjoys it. The taste no longer bothers him, and the feeling after the ritual is complete is better than he could possibly describe.

But when he turns and strides back into the cave, when he catches sight of Elena's dead body, that same pain tears through him. It hits him like a freight train, bringing him to his knees in the sand. Aiden has never felt anything like this in all his years.

What have I done?

In a dim room aboard the Jolly Roger, Cash is ready to give up on the pirate. He is so tired; his arms are not strong enough to keep up the compressions. Miles had to refill the warm water twice and tear up another shirt, but eventually the bleeding did stop, though it could be more that the pirate is dead, or close to it, rather than be due to their efforts.

Sure, Will's heart is beating, but is it Cash's doing, or will the pirate actually pull through? There is only one way to find out. Cash stops the compressions, flexes his fingers, stretches his arms over his head.

"Why have you stopped boy?" the first mate demands.

Cash rolls his neck. "The bleeding stopped, his heart is beating. Now, we must see if he is strong enough to survive."

Miles says nothing. Cash sneaks a glance over his shoulder at the man. The pirate is standing, arms crossed, glaring down at him.

"Truly," Cash holds up his hands. "There is nothing more that I can do. It's up to him now."

Miles stands firm for a moment before sighing. Uncrossing his arms, he rubs at his eyes with the palms of his hands.

"He is strong; he will make it," Miles says.

Cash merely nods, unsure of what else to say. He is saved from trying to find the words when another member of the crew cracks open the door, poking his head inside.

"We are approaching Skull Rock, sir. What shall we do when we make shore?" the man looks to Miles.

It is Cash who answers though. "We save Elena."

The man nods once and disappears.

"You will not win against Aiden alone," Miles says, looking down at the wounded captain. "He is too strong, especially if he has regained his magic."

"Then let's hope he hasn't," Cash states. "Where does the captain keep his weapons?"

For the first time in Cash's presence, Miles smiles.

~

Armed to the teeth, Cash steps off the gangplank and onto the shore of Skull Rock. He walks only a few steps before sprinting the remaining distance to the mouth of the cave. Was it really only a few days ago that he was tortured in this very cave? It feels like a lifetime has passed already.

The mouth of the cave comes into view. Cash can see the candlelight flickering on the walls, lighting the eyes up in a rather disturbing way. The closer he gets to the rock, the more he can feel death emanating from it. Cash prays he is not too late. With a sword already in his hand, he does not slow his pace as he enters the tunnel inside the mouth, as he rounds the slight corner and steps into the open area inside.

At first, he does not see anything aside from the stone slab in the center of the cave, but the sudden movement of Aiden's head draws Cash's attention. Aiden is kneeling in the sand, holding Elena in his arms. The king of Neverland is red from head to toe...is that *blood*? There are tears streaking down Aiden's cheeks when he looks up at Cash. It is then that Cash really takes in the entire picture. The long gashes down both of Elena's forearms, the dark stains in the sand. Cash's eyes land on Elena's face. She is as pale as a ghost, her lips so blue they are almost purple. No. It *is* blood on Aiden's skin, Elena's blood. *No!*

"What have you done?" Cash yells at the top of his lungs.

Aiden's shoulders heave as his unsettling green eyes

meeting Cash's. "I'm sorry." Aiden's words are choked with tears. "It was a mistake."

Outside, thunder booms in the distance. Cash can hear the wind picking up outside, the jungle rustling in response.

"You *monster!*" Cash shouts. Aiden hangs his head, forehead resting against Elena's pale skin.

"Get away from her," a voice growls from behind.

Cash looks over his shoulder to find Miles and a few other crew members soaking wet, standing at the caves entrance. Aiden does not move other than the slight shaking of his shoulders from his silent crying. Surely his emotional response is all a show. Miles shoves past Cash, stomping across the cave, sand spraying from his boots. Towering over Aiden, Miles looks down at the boy. Aiden looks so crushed, so helpless. Miles picks up one heavy boot and kicks Aiden roughly aside. He then kneels and scoops Elena up into his arms and turns, rushing out of the cave with the rest of the crew on his heels.

Cash spares a glance at Aiden, still lying on his side in the sand with his hands covering his face. He almost feels sorry for Aiden...almost. But then he remembers all that Aiden has done; he tortured him, he attacked the Jolly Roger and killed a number of the crew. The hole in Will's chest flashes through Cash's mind, then the wounds on Elena's arms, her blue lips and fingertips.

Tightening his grip on his sword, Cash steps forward. Aiden is vulnerable; he may be able to kill him, to end this. It will not change anything, nothing will bring Elena or Will back, but Cash will enjoy the feeling of revenge. Swinging his leg back, Cash kicks Aiden in the gut, then in the ribs. The king of Neverland writhes in the sand, hands still protecting his face. Before he can kick him a third time, Aiden vanishes.

"Kicking a boy while he's down," Aiden says from behind. "Bad form, mate."

Cash spins in the sand, sword already swinging, but Aiden is gone. Looking around the cave, Cash sees nothing but candles and blood. He swears under his breath, turns, and sprints back to the Jolly Roger. As soon as he is on board, the gangplank is pulled up, the sails are unfurled, and the ship slowly drifts away from the shore of Skull Rock.

Slowing his pace as he nears the quarters at the back of the ship, Cash shoves open the door to find Miles gently placing Elena's lifeless body on the bed beside Will's.

"Is he...?" Cash does not know how to finish his question. Miles straightens.

"He still breathes, which is more than I can say for Elena." The pirate's voice cracks on her name.

Cash looks at the two forms on the bed. Will is still pale, but nothing compared to Elena's pallor, and Miles was correct, the captain's chest still rises and falls. Squeezing his eyes shut against the tears threatening to spill from his eyes, Cash turns away.

"Is there anything that can be done for her?" Miles's voice is just a whisper.

"No," Cash sniffs, wipes his nose with his damp shirtsleeve. "Aiden bled her out completely, even if I did CPR, there's nothing for her heart to pump. She's gone."

A groan from behind has Cash whipping around, a spark of hope in his heart, but it is not Elena who is stirring. Will groans again, tries to sit up, collapses. His first mate rushes to his side.

"Do not try to move, Captain," Miles orders. "You are gravely wounded."

"Yes," Will responds, his voice even more gravelly than usual. "I can tell."

Miles smiles, but it does not reach his eyes. "Good to have you back, sir."

"Good to be back," Will offers his friend a small smile in return. When Miles doesn't reply, Will turns his head following the line of his first mate's gaze. When he notices Elena lying beside him, Will bolts upright, clutching his chest.

"No!" he roars. Will looks to Miles, then to Cash. "What happened?"

"We tried to save her," Miles holds his hands out, palms up. "We were not fast enough."

"No!" Will repeats the word over and over until it is an endless string. "Nononono!"

His hand hovers above Elena, above the wounds on her arms. He does not touch her though. Cash's heart hurts for the pirate, and for himself as well. Cash was so horrible to Elena after Will showed up in London, and most moments since. He should have forgiven her while he had the chance. It's not her fault that she was already in love with someone else when he finally had the balls to pursue her. Cash let his pride get in the way, and he will forever regret it.

The pirate opens his eyes to a blinding pain in his chest. A familiar form appears instantly at his side. Miles orders him not to move, as if he could not already tell that he was gravely wounded. When Will notices his friend's odd behavior, he follows the man's gaze only to find his worst nightmare has come true.

Elena is lying next to him. Her lips are blue, skin as pale as the whitecaps of the Never Sea's waves. It cannot be. The pain when he sits up is what he imagines being struck by lightning would feel like.

"No!" Will hears the word over and over. Is it his voice? It sounds so strange.

Will reaches out a hand but does not let his fingers touch her. Part of him is afraid; he does not want to feel the iciness of her skin. She looks so fragile, like just a touch could make her crumble.

"The boy," Will turns his cold gaze on Miles and Cash. "He lives?"

Miles nods in response.

"And he has full use of his magic again?" Will questions.

It is Cash that answers this time. "Yes, Aiden's powers have returned."

"Take me to him." Will demands.

"Captain?" Miles furrows his brows.

"Take me to him!" Will roars. Both men flinch slightly.

"Yes sir," Miles bows his head and turns, rushing from the room.

"Leave me boy," Will says to Cash before turning back to Elena's lifeless body.

"Will, I am so sorry," Cash says softly.

Will doesn't respond; he doesn't look at Cash or move at all. But when he hears the cabin door shut, when he is sure that he is alone, Will cannot contain the sobs that rack his body. Laying his head on Elena's stomach, Will lets his tears soak her grimy shirt.

On the island of Neverland, a storm rages, shaking the trees and mountains as Aiden steps into the clearing that houses his camp. The canopy is so thick that the downpour is a mere sprinkle. What is left of the fairies and children who accompanied him across the Never Sea have returned. Though none of the children perished in battle, many fairies' lives were lost. None so marked as Tatiana's though. A twinge of guilt mixes in with the pain in his chest. The thought that Tatiana will not flit up to meet him on his arrival or be waiting for him in his tree-house...it hurts. *What the hell is happening to me?* The boy wonders. Why is he feeling all of these things?

Aiden stops just inside the ring of trees surrounding the clearing and shakes his head from side to side. When his vision focuses, he sees the faces of his children and fairies looking back at him. The boy straightens and puts on his best smile.

"Congratulations are in order for a job well done, friends." Some faces smile back at him, others do not. "Our mission was successful, magic has been restored, all is as it should be."

The smiling faces nod while the others return to what

they were doing before he arrived. Some are lighting fires or cooking, some tending to their own wounds or others. Aiden says nothing more before lifting into the air and landing in front of his door.

Stepping into the small round space, Aiden looks around at what is left of the treasures he spent lifetimes collecting. Rage flows through his veins. He picks up the nearest trinket and dashes it against the wall. Shattered glass and metal ricochet onto the furs that cover the floor. He throws another, and another. It is not satisfying enough. Aiden closes his eyes and balls his hands into fists. The crown atop his head pulses once, twice. On the third pulse, every trinket and treasure in the treehouse explodes. Glass, metal and wood rain down to the floor. When it all settles, Aiden is standing in the center of the room, panting, nicks and cuts covering his body. One last pulse of the stones in the crown heals him back to perfection, and then their glow fades.

He does not bother cleaning up the mess before he exits the treehouse. Wary looks are cast his way as he descends and walks through the camp. The children who normally flock to him now cower away when he gets close. No matter, he does not need any of them, or their admiration. At the edge of the jungle, he pushes off and flies away, off to his favorite place on the island.

CHAPTER 11

"Do you think he'll be alright?" Cash asks Miles. The two are standing on the upper deck of the Jolly Roger, Miles at the wheel and Cash beside him.

"No," Miles sighs. "No, I don't think he will be. I don't see how he could ever recover from this."

Cash nods. Looking out across the sea, the large island is just beginning to come into view.

"What do you think will happen when we make shore?" Cash asks, looking back at the door of the cabin.

"Best case scenario, mayhem," the first mate shrugs.

Cash huffs a small laugh. "As entertaining as that would be to watch, I don't think Will can survive an altercation with Aiden in his current state, certainly not when Aiden has full use of his powers."

"Do not underestimate the captain," Miles shrugs. "Especially when it comes to that girl."

"He would do anything for her, wouldn't he?" Cash asks.

"Aye, you should have seen him when she left Neverland," Miles's eyes are vacant, remembering the time. "You have no inkling what he went through to get back to her."

Again, guilt invades Cash's insides. Elena and Will truly loved each other, maybe they were even soulmates. Now they will never truly know, they will never have a chance at the future they could have possibly had. A sort of resolve settles over Cash. He will help defeat Aiden, he will fight at Will's side and get revenge, not just for himself or Will, but also for Elena and what was done to her, because she can't get revenge for herself.

The waterfall is in ruins. This place was once his favorite in the whole of Neverland, but now it is just a mockery of the beauty that once existed. Boulders and debris are piled in the lake. What was once the biggest waterfall in all of Neverland is now just a trickle of water, choked by the destruction from the pirates attack on Elena's first night on the island. The cave where he kissed both Wendy and Elena for the first time, the only time he kissed Elena actually, is completely gone.

Rain pours from the sky and thunder rumbles in the distance as fresh rage fills Aiden. He does not bother using his magic to keep himself dry. He wants to feel the rain on his skin, hoping that it will drown out this fire burning inside of him, hoping that it will drown out everything that he is feeling.

The king of Neverland has never felt so alone. The feelings of guilt and anger have not been so strong since

Wendy's death. Aiden lays down on the plush jungle floor, the rain pounding on his chest and face.

What good is a king without his queen?

The Jolly Roger makes shore just as the sun is setting. Miles orders Cash to alert Will of their arrival, and to request orders. Cash knows that if Will goes into that jungle, if he faces his brother again, it will be suicide. But something tells Cash that nothing will stop the pirate captain from doing just that. Pushing the door open, Cash takes only a single step inside the dimly lit room. Will's head is resting on Elena's chest, just over her unbeating heart. At the sound of Cash's footsteps, Will bolts upright, clutching at his own chest. The cloth stuffed into his wound is red with fresh blood.

"I don't mean to intrude Will, but Miles sent me to tell you that we have made shore. What are your orders?"

Will closes his eyes, breathes in deeply. "Fetch my sword."

"Will," Cash protests. "I really don't think that would be a good idea."

Will's eyes snap open, they are like blue flame. They are so full of desperation and anger that it frightens Cash a little.

"I said, *fetch my sword,*" the pirate growls.

The motion of Will leaning forward causes him to suck in a breath through gritted teeth. Cash cannot hide the look of disappointment on his face. Will simply lifts his chin indignantly and looks away. Cash says nothing else;

he only turns on his heel and walks back out the door. Miles is still at the wheel, shouting orders at the crew. Pirates scurry around the deck like worker ants.

Cash comes to stand next to the massive man. "Will would like his sword, where is it?"

The first mate glances over briefly. "Aye, I assumed as much."

Miles pulls a brilliant looking blade from his weapons belt. How had Cash never noticed the beauty of it before now? The man hands Cash the sword. It is surprisingly light, much more so than the sword Cash was given. He turns the sword over, marveling at its scalloped edges, both beautiful and deadly. The entire blade is covered in intricate, beautiful carvings from the tip to the hilt. Speaking of the hilt...the biggest ruby Cash has ever seen is embedded in the pommel. Cash looks admiringly at the sword once more before turning away and heading back to the cabin.

"Boy," Miles calls out. "What are the captains' orders for us? What are we to do?"

"He didn't give any other orders," Cash calls back over his shoulder. "I believe he means to do this on his own," he adds quietly as he walks towards the closed cabin door.

Cash enters the room to find Will attempting to wrap his torso with part of the silky red sheet from the bed behind him. The rest of the sheet has been pulled up to cover Elena. Relief is the first thing Cash feels, followed quickly by guilt. He tells himself that it is normal to not want to look at a dead body. Especially the dead body of a girl he once fancied and then treated like garbage.

Will is struggling with his makeshift bandage. One hand and terrible wounds would cause problems, Cash imagines. Sighing, Cash walks to the desk, sets the gorgeous sword down and turns to Will with an outstretched hand.

"Let me help," Cash says.

"I don't need your help," Will hisses.

"Yes, you do," Cash insists. Will sighs now, but hands over the sheet. "You know this is a suicide mission."

"Aye," the pirate nods. "What's your point boy?"

"Dying won't bring her back," Cash presses one end of the sheet to Wills chest, signaling for him to hold it in place. He begins circling Will, pulling the fabric as tightly around the pirate as possible.

"No, but at least when I am dead, I will be with her again," Will spares a glance at the covered form on the bed. He averts his eyes quickly.

"How can you be sure of that?" Cash cocks one eyebrow and makes another pass.

"I can't," Will says. "Honestly, I'm more likely to end up in the underworld than with her, but I have to have hope."

"Fair enough," Cash admits. "Don't go alone though, let us come with you. Or Miles at the very least."

"No need for the rest of you to die for my revenge," Will says simply.

Cash sighs but doesn't argue further, Will has clearly made up his mind.

"There," he tucks the end of the sheet into itself, pulling it tightly through itself and tying it off. "I don't know how long that knot will hold, and I still don't think you should do this, but I'm finished."

"Thank you," Will turns to face him and places his hand on Cash's shoulder.

"For what?" Cash asks. "I failed. Elena is...dead. I failed her."

"No," Will's voice cracks. "*I* failed her. I was bested by the demon boy, it was my failure that allowed her to be taken, and it is all my fault that she is dead."

"No, no it is *not* your fault," Cash insists, but Will only waves his hand dismissively.

The pirate turns away, pulling a fresh shirt from a stack of clothing on the desk. It takes some time to maneuver himself into it. Will fumbles with the buttons for a few minutes before deeming his work good enough. Lifting the sword from where it lays on the desk, he slides it through the weapons belt still slung around his hips.

"I doubt that I will be seeing you again Cash," Will says. "So, I will take this moment to apologize to you. I am sorry that you ended up in this place, and that you will likely be stuck here now. I am sorry for all the pain that I have caused you."

Cash had not thought about that detail until now. What the hell will he do if he is stuck in Neverland forever?

"It seems as though we both have plenty to apologize for." Cash cannot hide the bitterness in his voice. He wants so badly to hate the man, but he can't.

"Yes, it seems that we do," Will agrees sadly. "Goodbye Cash. Believe me when I say that I hope we meet again."

Cash nods, lost in the thoughts rolling through his head. "Good luck, Will."

The captain walks out into the night leaving Cash alone in the cabin. Cash's attention is drawn instantly to the bed, to Elena's body. An uneasy feeling washes over him. He has seen more death in the past twenty-four hours than ever before in his life. The urge to run from the room is incredibly strong, but Cash resists. Instead, he walks very slowly to the bed and sits down. He reaches out a shaking hand and pulls the sheet down to expose Elena's face. It makes his stomach turn, but he does not look away.

"I'm sorry," Cash whispers. He is not stupid enough to believe she will hear his words, but he needs to say them anyway. "I'm sorry that I wasn't what you needed, and I'm so sorry for the way I treated you. I'm sorry that I was not strong enough to protect you, and I'm sorry that you are dead because of me." Tears roll down his nose and drip off the tip. Cash sniffles and wipes his nose on the back of his hand. Rising from the bed, he leans down to pull the sheet back up and walks out of the room without looking back.

Lying on the damp jungle floor, the boy stares up at a sky full of stars. He cannot get the image of Elena's corpse out of his mind. Her empty veins were barely visible beneath the pale, almost translucent skin. Those veins were empty and bloodless because of him, because of what he did to her, and his hunger for power.

Physically, he is back to normal, his magic restored to its full splendor. Inside though, he is falling to pieces. It is infuriating, this feeling. Never before has one of his sacrifices made him feel guilt, not even the botched or unsuccessful attempts. In fact, the only time he can remember feeling guilt at all was after Wendy's death.

His magic stirs at the thought of his first love. The

green glow engulfing his hands draws his eyes away from the stars. He snuffs it out with a tiny flick of his fingers. What is the point of having all this power if he feels all this guilt? He does not want to *feel* anything at all! The problem is, he cannot seem to stop it. He does feel; he feels for Elena, and now she is dead, just like his brother. They are both dead because of him.

If only there was a way to bring them back...

He knows that it is possible to bring someone back, but not more than one person, not even with his immense power. No amount of power would be enough to bring them both back.

The sound of footsteps pulls him from his thoughts. Who would be so bold to disturb him here? The footsteps draw nearer, and Aiden turns his head to find his brother stalking around the lake. It cannot be! He was dead! Then again, perhaps not, perhaps this is payment for all the things he has done. Is it finally time for him to face the consequences of his actions?

"Over here, brother," he calls out, lifting one hand in the air.

The pain is excruciating, but Will must power through. The smell of the sea fills his nose as he steps into the night. He stops and simply breathes it in for a moment, for it may be the last time he experiences it. Spotting Miles at the wheel, he goes to stand beside his friend.

"I fear this is goodbye old friend," Will says. "Your loyalty has meant—"

"I know," Miles interrupts. "Let me come with you, captain."

"No. I have to do this on my own," Will insists.

"Captain," the man tries again.

"Goodbye Miles. It has been an honor to sail the Never Sea with you these lifetimes." And then the pirate captain walks away, from his friend, from his crew, and from his ship.

The trek through the jungle in the middle of a storm is the worst thing Will has ever experienced. The purging of the darkness from his soul was painful, but this is so much more than just physical pain. Elena is dead. He will never hold her in his arms again, never kiss her, there will be no future for them. Will's chest aches and burns, and it is not just from the oozing wound.

Each step through the dense, dark jungle brings so much physical pain that Will thinks he may vomit, but he presses on. Each flash of blinding pain brings a vision of Elena. He sees the first time he ever laid eyes on her, flying past his ship laughing and so full of joy. He sees her face the night he first brought her to the Jolly Roger, streaked with tears. He remembers how she cried herself to sleep in his arms that night and how from that point on, he never wanted to be away from her. He sees their first kiss, when he knew that he loved her. By the time Will reaches the clearing that houses his brothers camp, the entirety of their relationship has played out in his head.

Pausing at the edge of the clearing, Will leans against a tree and takes a few deep breaths. He is exhausted, both physically and mentally. His head is crowded with visions of Elena's smile, with the sound of her laugh. At least when he is dead it will stop.

Pushing off the tree, Will walks slowly into the clearing. He has only seen his brother's camp a handful of times, and it is quite shocking how much it has grown. The largest trees surrounding the open space have treehouses built into their branches, most of them connected by simple rope bridges. Fairies and children alike occupy the camp. Groups of both are sitting around small fires, or roaming about, playing and socializing. The older children perform necessary tasks like cooking and laundry.

No one seems to notice him, and his brother is nowhere in sight. Will straightens his spine, though his wounds shriek with pain, and adopts the swaggering pirate façade that he has spent lifetimes perfecting. Creeping up to the nearest fire, he sees one of the older children meticulously stoking the flames. Quietly, he approaches the lad from behind, waiting until he is directly behind him to speak.

"Nice night for a fire isn't it mate?" Will says with a devilish smile.

The young boy jumps up from his seat on the log and whirls, holding a sharp stick out as a weapon. The terrified look on his face is priceless.

"W-what are you doing here?" The boy stutters over his words.

"No need to fear, I am not here for you," Will says with a flip of his hand. "Now, where is your king?" he adds seriously.

The boy takes a moment to recover from his shock,

twisting his face into a cocky smirk. "And if I don't tell you?"

"Well," Will says with a small laugh. "In that case, then you have every reason to fear." He holds up his hook knowing full well that he will not use it on the boy.

The child's face pales. "His favorite place, that's where he always goes."

It takes a few moments to sort through the information in his brain. Will doesn't know his brother very well, not anymore, but he does recall a day not long after they first arrived in Neverland. His brother had come to him, still so young and innocent, so eager to show Will the beautiful waterfall he had discovered. It figures that this meeting would take place where Will first saved Elena. It's the place where he pulled her from the lake, praying the whole time that he was not too late. That was the night that he carried her through the jungle, all the way back to the Jolly Roger. Will knew that very first night that he wanted to be with Elena. But now he is too late, Elena is dead, and this will be a much different sort of meeting.

Will rises from his spot at the fire with nothing more than a nod at the boy before walking back into the jungle. Once he is in the cover of the thick foliage, he drops his swagger, clutching at the wound in his chest. Now he must trek even further into the island. By the time Will gets to the waterfall, he will be so exhausted that he will not stand a chance against his brother. His death will surely be instant, though he wonders if that would be such a terrible thing. He cannot stop or turn back; he must push forward.

The sound of rain on the canopy above, an occasional rumble of thunder, and his own ragged breathing are all

Will can hear, the wildlife all sleeping or taking shelter from the storm. The jungle is so dark that he can hardly see five feet in front of him. He can also no longer smell the sea, instead the aroma of wet earth and damp vegetation are what fills his nose. Not nearly as pleasant as the salt and wind smell of the sea.

After what feels like hours, Will finally stumbles breathless onto the shore of a large lake. There is enough moonlight shining through the leaves above to see the destruction he and his crew left behind. It looks the same as he last saw it. There is even a cannonball embedded into the rock near the top of the waterfall. Will smiles slightly. It is only fair that he should destroy something his brother loved. Will scans the open space, but he does not see Aiden anywhere. Slowly, he begins to make his way around the lake, sword in hand.

"Over here, brother." Aiden's voice calls from somewhere across the water.

Then Will sees his brother's hand waving him over. He approaches cautiously, only to find Aiden lying on the ground, staring up at the sky.

"I see you survived," Aiden says.

"Aye," Will growls. "Though I cannot say the same for Elena."

Aiden sits up, hands out, palms facing up. "Will," he begins, but Will does not let him finish.

He presses the point of his sword into his brother's throat. "Do not speak, demon. You have done enough!" Will's shout echoes off the rocks. "How can you live with yourself? How do you justify killing these girls for your own selfish gain? Especially her, especially Elena!"

Aiden drops his gaze. "I know you won't believe this brother, but I am truly sorry. I regret it. All of it."

Will pushes the tip of his sword even further into the soft skin of Aiden's throat. "Then why? Why did you do it?" he demands.

"Because I'm a monster!" Aiden jumps up, knocking the blade aside and bringing his face close to Will's. "I let my hunger for power cloud my mind for too long, and during these lifetimes I lost myself and became this monster. And now I have lost *everything* because of it."

"And you have taken everything from me!" Will roars. "You will die for what you have done, but even then, we will still not be even." Will drops his sword, instead pressing the sharp point of his hook to Aiden's throat.

"You could have had everything brother. Me, Wendy, a long life, even if it was without your magic. We still could have spent lifetimes here together, all of us. If only you would have been satisfied with aging slowly instead of not at all."

Aiden's eyes burn into Will's. "You think I don't see that now? I see it all, I see what could have been, what I chose to throw away."

"Good," Will spits. "At least you understand why I am killing you." He presses his hook to Aiden's jugular, ready to rip out the throat of the boy who destroyed his life.

"I can bring her back!" Aiden says, squeezing his eyes shut.

Will's breath hitches. "No. No, it's not possible."

Aiden's eyes open again. "It is possible. Let me do this for you, Will."

"Why?" Will questions. "Why would you want to help me?"

"Because I am sick of being the monster," Aiden replies.

Will searches his brother's eyes but sees none of the malice or arrogance he is used to. He sees only regret and sincerity. Could his brother be that good of an actor?

"How do I know you're not lying?"

Pulling the ball of bloody fabric from the hole in his chest, Aiden drops it onto the ground before pressing his palm to the wound. A green glow emanates from his hand followed quickly by red hot pain. *This is it*, Will thinks, *he is finally killing me.* Looking down, he can see the muscle and skin knitting itself back together. Then the pain fades, and Aiden's hand drops back to his side. Will steps back, his hand roaming over the healed skin where only minutes ago there was a gaping hole.

"I can bring her back to you Will," Aiden promises. To prove his point even further, he takes the rudimentary crown off his head and drops it on the ground.

"Well then, we need to get back to the Jolly Roger." He smiles as hope blooms in his chest.

CHAPTER 12

The brothers do not speak for a long while as they trek through the jungle. The longer he walks alongside the brother that he spent so log hating, the more the hope Will felt is replaced by doubt. It creeps in with each step that brings them closer to the Jolly Roger.

"Can you truly do it?" Will asks. "Can you bring her back?"

"I believe so," Aiden nods. "Though I've never attempted it before."

Will nods and the two fall back into silence, but inside a war between hope and doubt rages.

The sound of the sea becomes audible after a while, signaling that they are nearing the end of their journey. Aiden stops abruptly and reaches out, grabbing Will's arm. Will spins around, the look on his face enough to make Aiden drop his hand.

"I regret it," Aiden blurts out. "All of it. Everything that has happened has been because of me, and I regret all of it."

For a moment, Will looks shocked at his confession. He presses his lips into a thin line, contemplating. "No," he finally says. "It was not all your fault."

"It was," Aiden hangs his head. "I have made so many mistakes."

"As have I," Will insists. "We have both played our parts for so long, brother. It is time to move forward."

Aiden considers his brothers words for a minute before nodding. "Yes. Yes, we should move forward."

Will turns away, setting off in the direction of the Jolly Roger.

"Wait brother," Aiden calls to him. "What do you say we make a bit of an entrance?"

It may be silly, childish, but he cannot resist. He spent the entire walk through the jungle going over what he must do to save Elena, and he cannot resist having one last bit of fun before he does what he has to. A few feet ahead, Will arches one brow at him.

"Shouldn't you be focusing on bringing Elena back?" Will asks, the disapproval obvious in his voice.

Aiden prickles at the words, but quickly shrugs them off. "I will get us there much more quickly *and* make an entrance," he grins before closing the distance between them, placing a hand on Will's arm, and lifts them both into the air.

"**H**ow long are we supposed to wait?"

Cash has been pacing the deck since Will left. It feels like hours have passed since then. At least the storm has stopped. Miles does not answer him, he only sighs and leans further over the railing.

"Are we just to sit here doing nothing until Aiden comes to kill us?" Cash questions the man. Again, no answer. "We should go after him; there must be something we can do help!"

"Boy," Miles growls, "calm yourself. He is coming back. Will is coming back."

"And if he doesn't? What then?" Cash is spiraling. He is terrified that he will never make it back home, and even more terrified that he will die on this island. His mother would never know what happened to him, he would never get to see his grandparents again.

"Then I suppose we—" Miles begins, but he does not need to finish the sentence.

"Perhaps you should have had a little more faith in me," Will says from behind Cash.

Whirling, Cash's face stretches into an involuntary smile. He did not realize how happy he would be to see the pirate back on the ship. But that's not all...the wound in Will's chest is completely healed, he is whole again.

"How are you healed?"

"That would be my doing," another voice says. And then Aiden walks up the gangplank and onto the deck, coming to a stop next to Will.

"What the hell is he doing here?" Cash and Miles demand in unison.

"He's here to help; he's going to bring Elena back," Will announces.

"Come again?" Miles asks at the same time Cash shouts, "You are not getting anywhere near her!"

"It is my only chance at getting her back," Will says.

"It could be a trick; you can't trust him!" Cash insists.

"Captain, I don't think— " Miles begins, but Will stops them both with one word.

"Enough!" he shouts. "If there is even the slightest chance that I can get her back, I will take it. Besides, she is already dead, what is the worst that could happen?"

"The worst that could happen is that we could *all* end up dead!" Cash wonders why he is the only one thinking rationally.

Will pushes past the crew, now gathered on the deck, drawn by the raised voices. "I don't care," he simply says as he walks towards the cabin at the back of the ship.

Aiden hurries after his brother, his eyes darting shiftily around at the men glaring at him. Miles and Cash glance at each other before following on their heels. Cash is not going to miss this, no matter how it turns out. Inside the cabin, Will has begun to light more candles. Aiden lets out a small laugh, and with a wave of his hand, every candle and lantern in the room springs to life. Will nods his thanks to his brother before slowly making his way to the bed, to where Elena's body lays lifeless covered by the crimson sheet. He pulls the sheet down, revealing her face.

"You did this," Will points a finger at Aiden. "Now fix it."

Aiden nods and gestures for Will to move aside, taking a seat on the edge of the bed when Will complies. Cash looks around at the faces of the men in the room. Miles looks warily back and forth between Will and Aiden, his hand on his sword. Will's eyes do not leave Elena's face. A bump from behind causes Cash to turn and see that the entire crew is crowded at the door, watching, waiting. Cash's heart is racing, his palms are clammy. Can Aiden truly bring her back?

Aiden takes a deep breath and places his hands on Elena, just over her heart. They begin to glow, the light steadily growing brighter as magic pours into her body, casting the room with an eerie shade of green that reminds Cash of poison. Cash cannot see Aiden's face, but he does see it when Aiden starts to shake. The tremors start in his hands and travel up through his arms, until his entire body is trembling. There is a bright flash and then Aiden collapses onto the bed. No one moves. Cash doesn't know how to react. Is Aiden dead? What the hell just happened? Then the most unbelievable thing happens...Elena gasps, draws breath, her eyes fly open, her hands clutching at her chest.

"Oh my God," Cash breathes.

"No boy, God has nothing to do with this," Miles mumbles.

Will rushes to the bed and takes Elena's face in his hands. "Elena!" he cries out. "Love, are you alright?"

"Will?" she gasps. "How are you alive?"

Will chokes out a laugh. "I could say the same thing of you!"

"What happened?" she asks. "Aiden, he— "

Cash can see it when Will remembers his brother. The pirate tears his eyes away from Elena's face to look to Aiden, still unconscious beside them. Elena follows his gaze, her own eyes growing wide with terror when she sees Aiden. She screams and struggles beneath Will, trying to get away. Cash has not moved since Aiden collapsed; he doesn't know if he has even breathed. He is not sure he even remembers how to.

∼

My lungs fill with air, my eyes open. The sensation is so strange that my hands fly to my chest, just to feel it rise and fall, to feel my heart beating. A face so familiar it could be my own appears above me.

"Will," my voice sounds odd in my ears.

How is he alive? How am I alive? I was dead. Will is about to explain to me how we are both alive when a look crosses his face. My gaze follows his, only to land on another familiar face. Aiden is lying next to me, eyes closed and not moving. His sweet and spicy scent assaults my senses and I can't stop from screaming. I want to get away, I try to get away, but Will is still kneeling over me. Panic spreads through my chest. My heart is racing, reminding me that it's a miracle it's beating at all.

"Is he dead?" I manage to ask.

Will has not moved or spoken. Then I realize there are other people in the room. Over Will's shoulder I spot Miles and Cash, and crowded in the doorway is the entire crew. No one moves a muscle.

"Do something," I say to no one in particular. "Will, do something!" I single him out this time. "Do something, damn it! You can't just let him die!"

That gets a reaction. Every head turns my way and every face is set in the same shocked expression.

"I'm sorry, what?" Cash is the first one to speak. "Did you just say we can't let him die? Elena, *he killed you!*"

Cash is right, Aiden killed me, he bled me out on an altar, and I *died*.

"He's Will's brother," I say weakly.

And for some very strange reason, I can't bear to watch him die.

"I'm guessing he's the reason I'm alive now too," I add, trying to justify my reaction.

I was going to kill Aiden myself, but now, even after all he has done, I don't want him to die. Will is still staring at his brother with the same look of shock. Cash presses his palms into his eyes before walking the few steps to the bed and pressing his fingers to Aiden's neck, checking his pulse. After what feels like forever Cash looks at me.

"I don't feel a pulse, and I don't think he's breathing," he says.

My heart stops all over again.

But then a miracle happens...Aiden bolts upright, gasping for air, making everyone in the room jump. Will grabs his brother's shoulder pulling him in for a hug.

"You did it!" His voice is so full of emotion; it tears me apart inside.

As Aiden begins to come to, he returns Will's embrace. I smile, thinking that finally, the brothers will have each other again, until Aiden's eyes meet mine over Will's shoulder. There is something different about Aiden now, and there is something extremely unsettling in his green eyes.

"You brought her back," Will continues, pulling back and smiling.

Aiden is still staring at me, but Will does not seem to notice. The urge to get away is so strong. I need to get out of this room, away from all the eyes staring at me. Inching to the edge of the bed, I turn away from the two brothers and set my feet on the floor. After testing my weight, I stand and mumble something about needing air before pushing through the crowd and out the door.

I walk all the way to the opposite end of the ship. Placing my hands on the railing, I lean out until I can see the carved figure that adorns the front of the vessel. When I lift my head, I realize that we are anchored on the coast of the big island. It's dark out, the jungle in front of me an impenetrable wall of blackness. Closing my eyes, I let the smell of the sea calm my nerves. It's my favorite smell in the whole world, something about it always brings me comfort. Leaning back and tipping my chin to the sky, I open my eyes. The sky is breathtaking, so full of stars, and the moon is so low I feel like I could reach out and touch it.

"Elena."

I'm so startled that I lose my grip on the railing and fall back, right into a pair of arms. Even if I hadn't recognized his voice, his scent would have given him away. Whirling, I find myself face to face with Aiden. He is looking down at me with that same intense look as he was in the cabin. I go to shove him away, but he grabs my wrists, pulling me in closer.

"What do you want?" I demand, struggling against his grip.

"It worked," he breathes, his grip on me tightening. "You're alive."

"How?" I stop struggling and stare up into his eyes. They are still bright and captivating, but different some- how. "How am I alive?"

Aiden turns my arms over and runs a finger up my

forearm where he had cut me open. The wounds are completely healed, there isn't even a scar.

"I used my magic to bring you back," he says softly. He is standing so close that I can feel the heat of his body. "It took all of it, but it worked, I brought you back," he continues.

It took all of it...

I pull back. "What do you mean?"

Aiden smiles, it is the saddest smile I have ever seen. "To bring you back, I had to give use all of my magic. There is nothing left."

I suck in a breath. "You gave up your magic? For me?"

He entwines his fingers with mine. "Yes," he says simply, dipping his head, bringing his lips close to mine.

"Why?" I can't breathe.

"Because Elena, you have awakened something in me that I thought could never be brought back. You made me feel again."

"Oh." It is the only think I can think to say.

Aiden's nose brushes mine, our breath mingles in the minuscule space between us. *This is wrong.* My eyes fly open. Yanking my hands out of his, I stagger backwards. He reaches for me, but I put more distance between us.

"Stop! I can't do this," I say crossing my arms across my chest.

"Elena please," Aiden takes another step toward me.

"Elena," Will appears behind Aiden, a wary look on his face. "What's going on?"

"Nothing, I was just coming to find you," I say. Starting forward, I try to go around Aiden, but he blocks my way.

Using my shoulder, I push past him but he stops me by grabbing my arm and pulling me back.

"Stay with me," Aiden pleads. "I love you."

My breath catches. I search those green eyes for something, anything, to show me that he is lying, that this is just another trick, another game. But all I see is raw emotion.

"You don't even know what love is," I say, jerking my arm out of his grasp. Turning away, I walk quickly to Will who wraps his arms around me.

"Are you alright?" he whispers into my ear.

I put on my best smile and look up at him. "Yes," I insist. "I'm fine, everything is fine."

He nods and smiles back but it does not reach his eyes. He knows me too well, but he does not confront me. Instead, he wraps an arm around my shoulders and begins to lead me away. Before we get to the door leading to the galley Will turns his head and calls over his shoulder, "Coming brother? I think we could all use a drink."

I don't look, but I can hear Aiden's footsteps as he follows us into the galley where most of the crew is already assembled. Well, those who survived Aiden's attack anyway. I don't know what happened to the bodies of the fallen men and fairies, and I don't think I want to know. Memories flash through my mind; seeing red, my rage and bloodlust as I cut my way across the deck to kill the brother of the man I love. That same brother killed me instead, then gave up the magic he killed me for to bring me back to life, then told me he loves me and basically begged me to be with him. I almost cheated on Will with him. I really am screwed up...

Will ushers me onto a bench and takes a seat next to

me. Miles sits on Will's other side and Cash across from us. Aiden walks into the room and everyone goes silent, all eyes are on him as he takes the spot next to Cash. Will takes a dented metal flask from Miles, swigs from it, and passes it to me. Without a second though I put the flask to my lips and gulp a few mouthfuls of the wine inside. It burns all the way down into my stomach. Passing it to Cash I watch him do the same; he doesn't even look in Aiden's direction when he passes it to him.

Aiden sips from the flask before returning it to Miles. Turning slightly, he looks at Cash.

"I feel as though I must apologize to you, for the way I treated you when you were my captive."

Cash snorts. "How about starting with an apology for taking me captive in the first place."

"Yes," Aiden agrees. "I apologize for that as well. And to you, brother," he looks to Will. "I owe the most apologies to you." "Aye," Will nods, taking the flask from Miles once more. "You do owe that to me, but more to Elena."

There is a hint of a challenge in Will's voice. The two brothers stare each other down until finally, Aiden drops his eyes to the table.

"Elena knows how I feel," is all he says.

"Does she now? And how *do* you feel?" Will slams the flask onto the table. Rising a little from his seat, he looks at his brother, challenging Aiden to confess his feelings for me. Placing a hand on his arm, I urge him to sit back down. This is not the time or place to have this conversation. I am so grateful when Cash starts speaking again.

"If you're as sorry as you say, then make it right, send us home," Cash finally turns to face Aiden.

"I'm afraid I cannot do that," Aiden says guiltily.

"Why the hell not?" Cash demands, slamming his hand on the table.

"It's not because I don't want to," Aiden looks him in the eyes. "It's just that I no longer have the ability to do so."

"What does that even—" Will starts to ask. Then the realization dawns on him. "You gave up your powers. That was the cost of bringing Elena back." It is more of a statement than a question.

"Yes," Aiden replies. "A small price to pay," he adds, looking at me.

Our gaze lingers on each other for just a second too long before I drag my eyes away. I should say something, thank him for sacrificing his power for me, for bringing me back, but I can't bring myself to say the words. It was his actions that led to my death in the first place, and while it is surprising that he made that sacrifice for me, I can't thank him for finally doing the right thing, not when it took so long for him to do so. Leaning into Will's side, I don't look at Aiden again.

Aiden clears his throat loudly. "As I said, I no longer possess the ability to send you back to London, but I can enlist a fairy to guide you home."

"Good," Cash nods and reaches for the flask now sitting on the table. "Make it happen." In my peripheral vision, I can see that Aiden is staring at me again, but I keep my eyes averted, looking at anything but him. I think he is waiting for me to say whether I will be joining Cash on the trip home, but that should be obvious by now. The real question is, is Will going to join me back in London? I would like to think without a doubt that yes, he will come back, but I also know how unhappy he was in my world. Then there is the fact that his brother is purely human again; that could give Will even more reason to want to stay. He said no to following me back once before, what will stop him from doing so again?

The rest of the evening is spent mostly in awkward silence. The crew eventually disappears one by one, some to sleep off the day's events, others to find a place to mourn the loss of their friends. Eventually all that is left in the galley are myself, Will, Aiden and Cash. Once the flask is empty, even Cash leaves us. The brothers remained civil to each other while the others were around, but in their absence the tension between them is undeniable. Will is the one to break the silence.

"Shall we retire, love?" he asks me. "It has been a rather eventful day."

I nod and rise from the bench, Will doing the same. Aiden pushes himself up as well.

"Ah, yes, well I'll leave you to it. I will return in the morning with a fairy guide that will take whoever wants to return, back to London."

I know the comment is directed at me, but I stay silent. Will nods and ushers me out of the room and onto the deck.

"Good night, brother," he says sharply.

We stay on the deck until Aiden has left the ship, then retire to our quarters. Will offers me use of the bathing chamber first so I grab clean clothes and start cleaning myself up. I am disgustingly filthy, and my clothes are little more than rags. When I remove my shirt, I look at my arm expecting to see the perfect handprint where

Tatiana burned me with her magic. The memory of her death is so jarring that I have to brace myself against the wall. I killed Tatiana, brutally. I slaughtered multiple fairies in my craze during the battle. I am a murderer. That thought, the events that took place here in Neverland, I will never be able to get them out of my head. I killed. I died and came back to life. Those are not things anyone could forget.

Stripping the rest of my ruined clothes from my body, I find that none of my wounds remain, nor are there any scars to show they were ever there. The magic that Aiden poured into me took care of all the major wounds as well as every nick and cut. I do my best to wash off all of the grime and blood from my face and hair in the basin before dunking a rag into the water and wiping down the rest of me. I desperately want a shower, but this will have to do for now.

After drying myself off and wringing out my hair, I go into the other room to find Will at his desk, pen in hand, writing something on a sheet of paper. When he realizes I am back, he quickly tucks the paper under a book and gets up. Planting a quick kiss on my forehead, he goes to take his turn to clean up. My curiosity gets the best of me; I can't help but pull the page out to see what he was writing. *Dear brother,* it starts, and I immediately put it back. My cheeks burn as the embarrassment washes over me for even looking in the first place.

Hurrying away from the desk, I lay down on the bed, instantly get comfortable despite the ruined sheets and close my eyes. I don't know how long passes, but eventually I feel Will sliding into bed next to me. He wraps his arms around me, pulling me close. He murmurs something in my ear, but I am too exhausted to listen.

I wake many times throughout the night. All I want to do is sleep but when I close my eyes, the darkness is far too like death. Everyone was so quick to point out that I died, but no one asked me the question I assumed they would. No one asked me what happened after I died. Maybe I'm the only one who ever wondered about what death was like, or what came after. Perhaps living such long lives in Neverland has skewed their thoughts about death. Or perhaps I am just weird and morbid. Death wasn't at all like I thought it would be though.

I knew that I was dying, I was ready to die. I was ready to be with Will again. But as I bled out on that altar in that creepy cave, I did not have the experience that I thought I would. There was the sensation of floating, like I was completely weightless, drifting in the sea. I remember feeling very warm, and I remember thinking that was odd. Movies and television shows always gave the illusion that you feel cold right before you die. Apparently, that was incorrect, at least in my case.

As the last of my blood drained from my veins, everything went black. And that is all there was, darkness. There was no montage of my life flashing before my eyes, there was no white light or pit of fire. There was just... nothing. It was pitch black, perfectly silent. It was terrifying. Every time I close my eyes I go back to that place, back to that nothingness. It scares the hell out of me, and I don't want to go back there. But I also don't want to talk about it, so in a way I am glad that no one has asked me what it was like.

The only good thing about being in that place was that I felt nothing. There was no pain, no hurt. It was just... nothing. I don't know how much time passed in that place, or exactly how long I was dead, it felt like an eternity. But then something happened. A green glow appeared. It started out very faint but grew quickly until the darkness was nothing but green. And as the light grew, I started to feel things again, I started to feel warm, my senses returned rapidly. It was like I was being pulled to the surface of the sea. Air flooded into my lungs and my eyes opened and suddenly I was back in the real world. Gasping, I let life fill me again, thanking the universe for giving me another chance.

I was dead, and now I am alive again. It's a miracle. Actually, it was magic, but either way, I don't intend to waste my second chance at life. My life is a gift now, and I will do everything I have ever wanted to do. I will love as hard as I can, eventually get married and have a family, build a career, travel. I intend to do it all; I just hope Will is by my side while I do it.

Will allows Elena all the time she needs to clean herself up. She has been through so much; it is the very least he can do for her. He takes the time to sort through the chaos in his own head. Aiden is no longer magical, nothing more than human. As long as he remains in Neverland, Aiden will age slowly, but that immortality and power he loved so much is gone. Aiden gave all of it up for Elena.

It is quite obvious how Aiden feels about Elena—Will saw enough on the deck earlier to confirm that suspicion. Elena's reaction to Aiden's advances was both heartbreaking and reassuring. She was tempted, but she resisted. Will knows that Elena loves him, that she will choose him, but he also knows that some part of her once cared for his brother. Maybe she still does.

Will feels the need to write his feelings down, and so he sits at his desk and pulls out a sheet of paper.

Dear brother,

I need to start by saying thank you. Thank you for sacrificing the thing you love most to bring back the thing I love most. I will forever be grateful for what you did for her, and for me. But I do know that it was not just for me that you did this, and though it was a very great thing that you did, it won't make up for everything. Performing this one act, no matter how large it may have been, does not make up for the centuries of wrong that you have done. But you are still my brother, so I say thank you.

I know that you love Elena as well. I saw how you looked at her tonight, how you touched her. I do not fault you for this, of course. Who could possibly resist loving her after all? While it seems that Elena has made her choice, if she ever does change her mind, I would not stand in the way of her happiness, even if that happiness lies with another.

I plan to leave Neverland with her tomorrow, and I do not intend on ever returning. But this is my invitation to you to come to London with us. It has been a long time since I have had a brother, and I would like to chance to get to know you again, so that one day we might possibly be a family once more. The only thing I ask of you is to not stand in the way of our happiness together, and in return, if she were to choose you, I will promise you the same.

I do hope that you consider this offer, Aiden. I have missed you, brother.

Yours,

Will

He has just finished signing his name to the letter when Elena emerges from the bathing chamber looking much cleaner, but utterly exhausted. Quickly, he tucks the letter away before she can read it. Not because he is trying to hide it, but because the things he admitted in it are things he is not entirely proud of. Like missing Aiden. Aiden has been a monster for so long that it should be impossible to see him as anything else, but Will still cares for him. He knows Elena would understand his feelings, but he tucks the letter away anyway before dropping a kiss on her head and going to clean up.

When Will returns, Elena is fast asleep. Quietly, he retrieves the letter, folds it and slips out to hand it off to Miles to deliver for him. He then slides into bed beside the love of his life and slips his arm around her waist.

"Sleep well, love," he murmurs into her ear. "One day, I intend to marry you, and I promise to spend my life making you the happiest woman alive."

She stirs slightly but does not wake. Will closes his eyes and slips into a deep sleep next to her.

~

The pirate arrives at Aiden's door not long after he himself does. The man says nothing, only hands him a letter and vanishes back into the night. Aiden's heart skips a beat, hope blooms inside of his chest. But when he reads the opening line of the letter, hope dissolves into disappointment. It is not from Elena, but from Will.

As he reads, a mixture of emotions flows through him. From disappointment, to anger, to joy. His brother managed to push every button he has. But to leave Neverland? To willingly travel to a world where he will quickly grow old and die? It is absurd. Aiden may not have his magic anymore, but if he remains in Neverland, at least the aging will be slow. He could have a century left, maybe even more.

Aiden tosses the letter aside, but his thoughts continue to stray to it all night long. Will made it seem as though there could be a chance for him and Elena. If he stays in Neverland, he will always wonder what could have been. And as small as that chance may be, is he willing to pass it up?

Aiden does not sleep at all that night; his mind is too full of chaos and choices. Instead, he spends his night pacing, but this time he is not plotting, he is debating with himself. To stay or to go, that is the question. A few days ago, he would never have considered leaving his kingdom. But now, without his magic, will it remain his kingdom? Elena is alive, Will is alive, there is a reason for him to hope again.

Living in London would present its own set of challenges of course. There would be the not so small matter of securing a profession. He wrinkles his nose at the thought, that does not sound enjoyable at all. And then there is the aging, which is even less appealing to him. If he is honest with himself, the only benefit of going to London would be Elena. Being close to her is the only reason he is even considering this. But even that chance is not enough to help him make this decision quickly. That's all it is, a chance, because Elena is with Will. She loves him. She *died* for him. That level of feeling is not easy to compete against.

He wonders if he is even capable of that kind of feeling...and the answer is no. No, he does not think he is. Elena deserves to be with someone who can love her properly, someone who can provide the best possible life for her, and he does not think that he is that person.

When the morning comes, Aiden looks around the clearing that has been his home for centuries. None of the children or fairies are awake yet, aside from the one fairy girl he enlisted to take them back to London, but Aiden does not wait to say goodbye. He walks out of the clearing and begins his trek back to the Jolly Roger.

I feel better when I wake up the following morning. I am exhausted from the lack of sleep, the dark dreams still swim at the back of my mind, but nothing hurts. My wounds are fully healed. It's like I've been remade, reborn. Sitting up in bed, I stretch my limbs, enjoying the sensation of the sheets on my skin, the smell of the sea and of

Will, still sleeping beside me. Today I feel good, and we are going home.

Slipping carefully out of bed so I do not disturb Will, I crack open the door and emerge into the brilliant early morning sunlight. Only a few members of the crew are up and about. Strolling across the deck, I soak in the sunshine, the air. I will miss this place, but I am ready to go home. At the front of the ship, Aiden stands, leaning out over the railing just as I did last night.

Part of me still screams to run away when I see him, but he is just a boy now. Even so, I approach him slowly. Leaning on the rail beside him, I look over.

"Good morning," I say politely. He must have been lost in thought because he jumps at the sound of my voice.

"Oh, good morning Elena," he returns my greeting.

"You're here early," I observe. There are dark circles beneath his eyes, did he sleep at all last night?

"I figured that you would be eager to get home," he replies, rubbing the back of his neck.

"Yes, I am." There is a very long silence after my reply.

Finally, Aiden opens his mouth to say something, but is cut short by Will, who sidles up next to me, nods to Aiden and drops a kiss on the top of my head.

"Did you consider my offer?" Will asks. I look questioningly at him, but he ignores it.

"I did," Aiden shrugs. "But I will be better off here in Neverland."

"If you say so," Will shrugs. "Are you ready to go home?" He directs the question at me.

I can't stop the grin that spreads across my face as I nod eagerly.

Will smiles down at me.

"Then let's go home."

He steps aside to reveal Cash standing a few feet away with a little fairy girl perched on his shoulder.

I start to walk away but turn back and embrace Aiden. His sweet and spicy scent fills my nose as I hug him tightly.

"Thank you for bringing me back to him," I whisper into his ear. "I wish you nothing but the best, Aiden."

Releasing him, I turn again and do not stop this time until I have reached Cash and our fairy guide. I watch the brothers speak for a few moments before awkwardly embracing each other, and then Will joins our little group. The fairy sprinkles her dust on us and we begin to rise into the sky. She sets us to the correct course and begins to head towards the second star to the right. Before I follow, I spare one last glance down at the Jolly Roger and at the boy watching us from the deck. And then we are gone, rocketing up into the stars.

The boy wanders through the jungle until he reaches his favorite place. Circling the lake, he bends down to retrieve the crown from the ground where he dropped it. When he places it atop his head, the stones do not pulse with magic, but he felt odd not wearing it.

Sadness fills the boy. He is sad for the loss of his magic, for the loss of his brother, and for the loss of Elena. Such feelings are foreign to him, that will certainly take some getting used to. But he is a clever boy, and he will persevere all the same.

High above the city of London, a boy with strange green eyes perches on a throne of deep grey rain clouds. His eyes search until he finds what he is looking for. At a table far below, a woman with beautiful auburn hair sits with a dark-haired man and a man with honey colored curls. They look much older than the last time he saw them, but then again, he has aged a bit himself.

He watches as they talk and laugh with each other, enjoying the lovely warm weather. He watches until the three get up and go their separate ways, the man and woman pushing a stroller down the road, and the honey haired man leaving alone.

The boy smiles to himself, though his heart is filled with sadness at what could have been. Many times over the years he found himself wishing he would have chosen differently, but he cannot change the past. And so he nods to the fairy perched a few feet away who sprinkles him with dust, for that is the only way he can fly now. With one last look at the couple strolling down the street, the boy smiles and turns to the fairy.

"Alright, let's go home."

ABOUT THE AUTHOR

Nicole Knapp is originally from California, currently living in Oklahoma. She loves to read and write Young Adult Romance, fantasy, and the classics. The Missing Piece is available from Amazon in paperback and Kindle version. Hook & Crown, a dark and twisted retelling of Peter Pan, is set to release in Autumn 2019 from Parliament House Publishing.

AIDEN, ELENA, & WILL NEED YOUR HELP!

Did you enjoy Stars & Steel? Reviews keep books alive . . .

Aiden, Elena, and Will still need you! Help them by leaving your review on either GoodReads or the digital storefront of your choosing.

Thank you!

ACKNOWLEDGMENTS

First off, I have to say thank you to The Parliament House Press for taking a chance on me and on this story. They saw the vision of Neverland that I pictured in my head and have truly helped bring it to life. Thank you, Shayne, Chantal, and the entire team for believing in this story as much as I do. Extra thank you's to my lovely editors for putting up with me throughout the long process of finishing this book!

Next, I want to say thank you to all the people closest to me who have spent the past few years cheering me on while I worked on these books. I am so grateful of their support. Without the hours they spent brainstorming with me, working through plot-holes, and talking me off the ledge when editing and writing got tough, these books would not exist. I couldn't have done it without all of you. I love you, all.

But most importantly, I want to say thank you a million times over to my readers. You are the real reason that I was able to finish this series, and you all are the reasons that I continue to write. If my work can bring enjoyment to even one person's life, then it makes the hard times and struggles all worth it. I am eternally grateful for each and every one of you. <3

www.ingramcontent.com/pod-product-compliance
Lightning Source LLC
Chambersburg PA
CBHW061449210726
48287CB00007B/2423